TRAIN
THOUGHTS

D1502114

JAY SIGLER

Train Thoughts

For more information:

Website: www.TrainThoughtsBook.com
Facebook: www.facebook.com/TrainThoughtsBook/
Twitter: @train_thoughts
Email: train.thoughts.book@gmail.com

Edited by Emily Schein

Book and Cover Art by Rachel Garrison
Twitter: @octabat
Email: octabat@gmail.com
Instagram: www.instagram.com/octabat/

Graphic Design and Layout by Jeff Dometita
Email: jeff@minuetproductions.com

Book Formatting by Derek Murphy @Creativindie

ISBN-13: 978-1985802421 | First Edition: April 2018

For Evan and Ella

Chapter 1

THE SECOND LONLIEST DAY OF MY LIFE was the day I lost my Vicky. The loneliest day of my life was after her funeral, surrounded by family and friends. The reception. I walked across the faded wooden porch into the house that used to be our home and mourners swarmed to me like flies to shit. My misery did not love company. I wanted to be left alone, so I could get back to dying alone. Instead, I was the center of attention and everyone did a fairly decent job of being concerned. The forced empathy these people were programmed to display was as transparent as the plastic wrap covering the food they brought. They were only there because that's the price you pay when you label yourself "friend" or "family." Ten minutes after leaving it would be, "Poor guy. Now, what do you want for dinner?" and their lives would continue as planned. No one really cared and I was getting sick of the heart-piercing condolences sharpened for situations like this. Somewhere amidst the stabs of "We're so sorry" and "Let us know if there's anything we can do," I was trapped between a table full of comfort food and the rest of my life. Everything from roast beef to chocolate cake sat on the table as a failed attempt at consolation. The food was supposed to make it easier, but it only filled stomachs. I could eat the whole fucking buffet and still be empty.

I loved my wife with all of my heart, with every breath I took. She was my best friend for ten years and now she was gone for even longer – forever. It felt like someone had punched through my abdomen, grabbed my stomach, and squeezed until pockets of air and bile ballooned through their clenched fingers. The dry, gagging feeling in the back of my throat couldn't be remedied by vomiting since my stomach was clamped so tightly. This feeling became my normal state of being every moment I thought about my life without Vicky. I was lost without her and had no idea how to continue living or if I even wanted to. What I did want was these people out of my house, but there's no sharp, polite saying that gets people to leave so you could ponder the best way to kill yourself.

On the outside, I did a decent job keeping it together for the duration of the event. There were fake tears in all the right places, conjured up for those who told me it would get easier with time, or some other equally unprovable theory. These tears were more for their benefit than mine. Seeing me cry in their presence made them feel they did their duty as the widower comforter. I saved the real ones for later when I was by myself. But for those three hours, I sat stoically and listened to everyone else reminisce about all of their memories of my wife, except for the most recent one about how she left us. That memory they avoided. And maybe it was selfish on my part, but I didn't care what they had to say. As soon as they walked out the door, Vicky's memory would be just that – a memory. They wouldn't have to deal with the agonizing pain of endless reminders staring them in the face with every waking moment. That torture was just for me.

The bathroom cabinets still full of Cover Girl makeup that would never be used, but that I couldn't yet bring myself to throw out. Sticks, brushes, swabs, gels, bottles, a collection full of colors, when all I saw was black and white, the Before and After. Desert Mist tan eye shadow applied over a True Blend Natural Creamy 420 foundation would never highlight her high cheekbones and petite jaw. Bright red Shine Blast lip gloss would only ever paint memories. The Conair curling iron still had shoulder-length strands of burnt brunette hair stuck in it. The empty chair once used to navigate these tools would never again be draped with the pink microfiber bathrobe that took too much effort to properly hang up when damp. Today's Woman magazines turned up in the most random places in the house, reminders of how a woman should live. The clinging remnants of her Tommy Hilfiger Freedom perfume hung faint in the air while I got ready for work. I could still taste the citrus and green florals that I would never smell fresh again. The only new thing I smelled was the sickeningly greasy roast beef that stained the air with its putrid stench. A smell I would forever associate with utter despair.

The smell had a different effect on the guests and the food lasted until everyone had their fill of comfort. After a few hours, my friends and family had stayed as long as predetermined for this type of situation, "family" staying slightly longer than "friends." One by one, every person slipped out of the house and out of my life, each with a saying that could make millions if only copyrighted and stuck on a Hallmark card. The promises to keep in touch were as believable as any religion's promise of salvation. It sounded nice but there was nothing to validate that it would ever happen. That was fine with me; I just wanted them gone.

When the door finally shut the last person out, I physically caught up to where I was mentally. Alone, I crumbled to the kitchen floor and cried. Hot tears mixed with hotter snot ran off my face and into the deep, narrow holes in the floor where she had last lain. I flashed back to the image of her lying there as I found her. I screamed and cried and dry heaved nothing but acidic bile from stomach muscles clenched painfully tight. As I gasped for breath to avoid choking, a million thoughts, feelings, and memories surged through my mind like a pulsing electrical current through a wire. Between each surge, I prayed for death. My wife was taken from me in such a horrific way and I was left with only myself and my thoughts. Shrouded in a cloud of pain and misery, I grasped at ways to get through what had happened. Vicky once told me that the mind is like a very powerful machine, so powerful it can get you through anything. I turned this phrase over and over in my head that night and the dark cloud of misery started to shift. I thought I saw a way to get through this.

Chapter 2

The idea of boarding a train to anywhere else and starting over was as refreshing as lemonade on a hot summer day. I could begin a new life where no one knew me and what I had been through. No one would know I was a widower and tip-toe around me like I was some fragile porcelain doll. No one would pretend to care, offering programmed responses thrown out solely for my benefit. I could start over. I could buy a train ticket to anywhere and simply forget my wallet, my keys, and my wife. Well, I did just that. Except I forgot to forget my wallet. And my keys. And my wife. I forgot to forget everything. The only part of my plan I stuck to was boarding that train. And I just ended up at work again.

The train is best described as a packed sardine can filled with people I don't care about who don't care about me. Each car on the train is set up so it jams the largest number of people into the smallest area possible. Given my background in mathematics, I already know this is the car's length times width times height divided by the approximate length times width times height of each person. Though whoever figured this out for the train company assumed either children or vertically challenged people were the only ones who rode the train. There is no personal space for the vast amount of strangers forced to temporarily coexist with each other.

Seats on the car are split between two levels. On the bottom level, there are two rows of blue padded benches separated by an aisle that runs the entire length of the car from door to door. The squeaky backs of each bench can be moved so that both seats of the bench face in the opposite direction. Families do this to set up pods, one bench facing forward, and one facing backwards, four seats facing each other. It's the closest thing to isolation you can get in this cramped environment.

On the upper level of the car, there are two rows of single padded seats separated by empty space that look onto the lower level. These seats span only half the length of the car and, like the benches below, the seat backs can be moved to face in the opposite direction. The other half of the car's upper level is a row of single seats running along the wall of the car, perpendicular to the train's motion. Sitting in this section, you are forced to face the person sitting on the opposite side over the empty space in the middle.

To get to where I work at Numerical and Systems Data Analysis, a two-hour train commute from the suburbs to the city consumes a sixth of my life. In this time, I've discovered that I am an upper-level person. I like knowing that it's going to be me and only me sitting in a seat, instead of dealing with random people coming and going at different stops. I like consistency. You could probably even tell which day of the week it was just by which shirt I had on. I tried sitting on the bottom for a few weeks when I first took the job and had to deal with everything from obese women smashing me into the window to elderly men taking a nap on my shoulder. The bum that made me smell his tangled long hair and soiled clothes for the entire duration of the ride was the last straw. But in order to get the privacy of the upper level seats, you need to get to the train early. Even if you're a few minutes late but lucky enough to find a spot in the second half of the upper level, you're still stuck facing another person, having to acknowledge that there are other people in this world.

Chapter 3

Alone in that tin can for four hours a day, I used to read books on theoretical physics or discrete mathematics, anything I thought would keep me sharp for work. After the funeral, though, the time was used solely to think about the death of my wife and contemplate nothing but unanswerable questions. Why did this have to happen? I hated the person that took her life. Why did it have to happen on a night when I worked late and wasn't there? I hated myself. Why is it that the police and detectives have no leads in the gruesome murder of my best friend and companion? I hated everything.

In an attempt to pass the time with something other than the pain and misery of these questions, I picked up the hobby of watching people on the train. Out of what was once a random existence of people, patterns began to emerge as soon as I started paying attention. The habits I observed in individuals were so consistent, I found myself piecing together the back stories of their lives. The trick was to remember that these were people I didn't know and didn't care about, which proved to be more difficult than it seemed. Vicky was right. The mind is a very powerful machine and in my intensely lonely mind, these people became my friends.

The second week after the funeral, I was back at work and the train was filled with three of my best friends that I'd never met: Sheila, Neil, and Frank. Learning their real names through hours of listening to their conversations made our friendship much more personal than just calling them Obese Woman, Old Guy, and Mr. Nice. They were already in their seats before I even stepped foot in the tin box. I had been at home deciding between white or wheat toast and between orange juice or killing myself. My choice was obvious for anyone paying attention. I still had white bread crumbs on my shirt. I took my single seat facing forward on the second level. Directly in my line of vision of the bottom row sat my friends, Sheila behind Neil, and Frank behind both of them, another typical day.

Sheila sat by herself since she took up more than half of the space on the bench. She was an overweight woman in her early to mid-forties if I had to guess. Sections of her jet black hair had started to gray so she kept it pulled back in a tight bun to hide it. This trick might have worked for her friends on that level, but not for me. From where I sat, my bird's eye view saw the gray hair spiral out from the top of her scalp into her bun like swirling flushed toilet water.

When I looked at her face I saw that at one point in her life she was the most popular cheerleader in high school. She used to be beautiful, but had eaten too much comfort food at too many events. Perhaps greasy roast beef at sad events, maybe the cake at happier ones. Her chubby, oversized body was the price she had paid for being so popular and attending so many events. The greasy complexion of her skin and the raised bumps of acne suggested she didn't have the slightest idea that eating whatever she wanted would eventually catch up to her. The greasy complexion of the McDonalds bag in her hand suggested that she still didn't know. Every morning I watched her stuff her face with sausage biscuits, Egg McMuffins, and hash browns that came out of paper wrappings so soaked with grease, I saw what she was going to eat before it was even unwrapped.

Despite her weight, Sheila had attractive albeit morose green eyes. The few times they passed over me, seeing me only as part of the scenery, I detected a definite sadness in them. Lonely shards of emeralds, they desperately sought to be a part of someone or something. In the way a light bulb will get extremely bright just before burning out, her eyes were stuck at the cusp of this brightness, one step from being forever gone, and it reminded me of the reflection I saw in the mirror each morning.

Her partner in crime, Neil, sat in the bench right in front of her every day. He was what the Marlboro Man would look like fifteen years after missing the memo that cigarettes were no longer cool. The deep wrinkles in his just-as-deeply-tanned skin suggested years of working an outside job, probably construction, given his broad shoulders. Pure white hair matched the single diamond earring glinting in his left ear, one of his two attempts at staying young. The other was trying to impress Sheila. His rough, rumbling voice practically growled out every word, letting you know how tough he really was.

"Lookit what my boat did to my ring this weekend," he blurted, shoving an oversized gaudy golden ring right under Sheila's nose. "I was tyin' the damn thing to the dock and the knot slipped and scratched the fucking thing." There was a formula to all of his stories. They all involved his boat and some expensive trinket, anything that deferred focus away from him being the only character in them. Last week I had heard about the terrible reception his new cell phone got, preventing him from notifying the Coast Guard of the school of sharks he swore he saw. I wondered if these grandiose stories were his way of accepting his own loneliness or his way of ignoring it.

"Aw! No way! That's too bad. Can you have it fixed?" Sheila responded between mouthfuls of food, both of them ignoring the tiny piece of egg that had flown out of her mouth and stuck to the window between their seats.

"Fucking hope so. Earned this ring in college playing football. It's not like I can just buy another one."

"Yeah, and it's safe to say you're a little too old to get back into college and earn another one," Frank chimed in with a grin from his row behind them. When Frank smiled, it looked like he was crying. The worry lines all over his face were dug-out trenches that lead to nowhere. Slumped shoulders and a permanent turned-down mouth hinted at a hard life filled with people walking all over him, both physically and mentally. The deep lines that crossed his face like a spider's web weren't the only display of his stress. The remaining tufts of hair over his ears were a thin nest housing a shiny eagle's egg waiting to be hatched. Despite all of his physical implications, he greeted everyone on the train as if they'd been through some life changing event together. I never understood how someone could constantly be so positive after a life of such obvious torment.

"Real funny, tough guy. You think I couldn't still kick some of those college kids' asses? I'll let you know there's quite a few I'd be sending home crying to their mammies," Neil responded with a smirk on his face, glancing over at Sheila to make sure she heard. She did. She nodded in agreement, or maybe it was in encouragement, or maybe she was just chewing.

"I know, I know, Mr. State Champ. Just pulling your leg. Happy Monday, guys." Frank shook his head from side to side, smiling at his own teasing. He always managed to nod and laugh in the right places.

"You too, Frank," Sheila said, following it up by jamming half of a hash brown into her mouth. "I hope you had a good weekend. Do anything special?"

"Not so much. The boss needed me to come in on Saturday and part of Sunday. Our group fell a little behind and we needed to make it up." Seeing the look of pity on Sheila's shaking head, he continued, "Don't give me the speech. I know what you're going to say. I should have stood up for myself. It's okay, though. He knows I'm a hard worker so I was the team's best shot at getting caught up."

"Make sure you clean your toenails while you're bent over, grabbing your ankles there, buddy," Neil offered up, explaining the situation quite accurately.

      Similar banter happened like this every day, usually for the entire duration of the trip. What I didn't actually hear, I filled in from my own imagination. I got the gist. Despite their own personal hardships they were all in good spirits for each other. Neil knew that Sheila needed to listen to someone, so he shared his stories with her. Sheila knew that Neil wanted to stay young and impress anyone through all of his adventurous stories, so she listened and was impressed by him. Frank knew that both of them needed a friendly greeting or a joke and they both knew Frank needed someone to pay attention to him. What they had, their train friendship was good for them. It worked. It was their everyday therapy for dealing with the everyday problems in their lives outside of the train.

Chapter 4

About halfway through my commute to work we picked up more of my friends. They were actually two friends for the price of one, "The Happy Couple." Gina and Rob. They were my closest friends, not only because they sat right in front of me, but also because I overheard all of their whispered conversations. Hearing these secret conversations not meant to be shared with others made it a much more personal friendship. There were no rings on either of their hands, but I assumed they'd been romantically together for quite a while by the way they kissed after getting off the train. It wasn't the long, passionate kiss of a new love, but more a comfortable, familiar peck. Gina would automatically extend up on her toes to meet Rob's hunched-over looming face so that both lips hit their mark without any hesitation or thought.

Rob was tall and skinny with narrow black-framed glasses that did nothing to remove attention from his receding hairline. The square lenses magnified eyes that were too far apart, resembling a bug's when you faced him. He always had a smug grin on his face that told everyone he knew he was better than them. He interacted with Gina like he tolerated her, as opposed to listening to anything she said. He always wore a suit with black Converse sneakers. I wasn't sure if they were for walking through the muddy streets in the morning or his personal statement of how hip and cool he was. If given the chance to actually meet him in real life, I would most likely just ignore it. I only considered this cocky man my train friend because of his lovely companion, Gina.

Gina, by contrast, was very short with red hair twisting down to her shoulders. The thick and tight curls reminded me of the type of pasta Vicky used to cook for dinner. Gina's shocking green eyes reminded me of two shots of Apple Pucker balanced on cheeks dotted lightly with freckles, reminiscent of a Raggedy Ann doll. At this time of year, her outfit was covered by a cream-colored jacked pulled tight, failing to hide the curves that made me understand what Rob saw in her. Despite her man being a smug prick, she obviously wore the pants in the relationship.

"Rob, did you remember to empty the dishwasher last night?" she asked from behind accusing eyes on the day they unknowingly became my friends. They both sat on the upper level directly in front of me, facing each other, for a daily date.

"Yeah, Gina, I did," he said with an eye roll and a slightly skewed nod backwards that really meant, "Here we go again."

"Well, if it was empty, why did you leave your dishes in the sink, instead of putting them in the dishwasher?" she whispered through an indoor voice that came complete with individually accented words. That made her question so much more important.

"Because I was looking for ways to piss you off, I guess." He looked around from between slumped shoulders to see if anyone else noticed him getting a scolding and could share in his misery. "That's what I do. I sit around thinking, 'You know, Rob, what would piss Gina off? You should do that', and then I do it."

"You're such an asshole. Seriously."

I enjoyed these daily exchanges of words, because I used to be Rob experiencing this humiliation. I would get in trouble for letting the garbage bag get so full it would tear. It seemed like Vicky would wait until we were in front of a large group of people before playfully informing me how terrible I was. It used to drive me nuts, being put on the spot like that. I would play along, acting like my life was so miserable, but I really wasn't miserable and neither was Rob. Given the choice of being yelled at by the person I loved or sitting alone at night dealing with the desolate pit my existence had become, I would never do the fucking dishes again.

Chapter 5

I've worked even more since Vicky died. Preoccupation with my job is what kept the rubber band of my sanity stretched tight around my head, preventing it from slipping higher and tighter, eventually leaving forever in a quick snap. I worked around eighty-five hours a week crunching numbers as a Numbers Analyst, the logic being that if I thought about numbers I couldn't think about people, alive or dead. Surrounded by numbers, I was never alone. And numbers don't die.

My job at the lab where I work basically boils down

to figuring out what "X" is in a given equation. The equations themselves usually look like a baby took a mouthful of alphabet soup and vomited it onto a piece of paper. They are handed down to us from whoever is the next rung higher on the corporate ladder. I can only assume this is my boss, Mr. Stark, not that I ever see him. My work usually presents itself in some form of email or online spreadsheet that I have to fill out. When I first started in this business so many years ago, we used the obsolete tool called paper. Once or twice a year, I am graced with an in-person appearance of Mr. Stark to get my review, but other than that, he's just a first and last name in my inbox. For further separation, the higher up the corporate ladder you climb, the higher floor in the building you get to reside on, so there is never any reason to come down to our floor. Another example of someone I don't know and don't care about.

In addition to the mysterious management system here at work, the reasons the equations need to be solved were never quite explained. Our only instruction is to figure out X. Sure, I knew Boltzman's Constant was used heavily in thermodynamics, entropy was the measure of disorder in a closed system, and energy was measured in joules, but what the result was to be applied to, I never knew. I could be feeding the hungry or balancing the national debt. I could also be creating bombs or figuring out the maximum price to sell DVDs at Wal-Mart. The end result – how to cure cancer. But the reason I like the job is because each equation has a definitive answer. You are given Y and told to figure out X. There are mathematical rules based on logic and if you followed them precisely, you are given a result. It was pretty much the only thing that still made sense in my life.

Like last week, I planned to bury myself in the numbers, to again hide in my office, lock the door, and appear too busy playing catch-up to be bothered. I was wrong.

"Do you want to eat lunch outside with me today? Get some fresh air and take your mind off of things?" Julie asked. I could tell her sympathy from two weeks ago had continued on to the workplace. "I just can't believe you're back so soon after.....you know...so soon. It's only been like a few weeks."

Julie was most guys' dream, but her fiancé's reality, tall and blonde with a body hitting all the right numbers. Both gorgeous and smart to boot, she was constantly reading classic literature and pursuing a psychology degree via night classes at the local university. All this in addition to figuring out X. She was my closest acquaintance at work and I'm not sure why. When we first met, I thought she was just a nice person who wanted to include everyone she could in her life. But over the past five or six years, we've become pretty close as far as work associates go, sharing the latest gossip about who was doing whom or thinking about quitting.

I politely shook my head no and told her I was too busy for lunch.

"You know, according to Jung, your energy well is dry. Your psyche is telling you to sit up and start paying attention to something in your life."

I told her it wasn't that, I was just really busy, but knowing a slew of remarks were about to be thrown at me like darts at a dart board anyway, I pretended to catch each one with my fingers so I could count them.

"We're just so worried about you."

Thumb pierced.

"If there's anything I can do, just let me know."

Now the pointer.

"I'm so sorry for your loss."

Pinky stuck.

"You shouldn't be back at work so soon."

No need for rings.

I remained silent while I shook my head no. The only thing I had to say was said as I waved goodbye to her back with my last remaining finger.

27

Chapter 6

That night, I arrived back at the house that used to be my home and ignored all the messages that were blinking at me on the answering machine. Unless there were payphones in the afterlife, I had nothing to say to anyone. I threw a frozen dinner into the microwave without caring what variety of processed shit I would soon be eating. For the next four minutes of my life, I was reminded of Vicky's death in the absence of her daily chatter. I tried to fill the space by telling her how my day was.

"I went to work today and Julie came to my office

again. We had to figure out the volume of a spherical cone as applied not only in Cartesian coordinates, but also in radius and degrees. The main crux was that the cone was expanding and contracting as a function of time."

The only response I got was the microwave beeping to me that its work was done. I took my burnt meal out of the microwave, barely feeling the tips of my fingers blistering from the cardboard. As I ate, I noticed the house was a lot darker. I had only been using lights that I absolutely needed on; the fewer reminders that at one point I had a happy life filled with joy and love, the better.

After dinner, there was not much to do but watch two-dimensional images flicker their life lessons at me, perfectly solved scenarios occasionally interrupted by a laugh track. Like pity, the laugh track was only another programmed response I had to deal with - it didn't even matter if the joke was funny or not. It's amazing the shit people do just because they are told. Vicky and I used to mock these laughing drones by coming up with our own varieties of laughs and using them for the rest of the show. It was one of the many foolish games we played to amuse ourselves. I remember she came up with one laugh that can only be described as a guffaw. The high-pitched, "Heeeee Haaaaaw Heeeee Haaaaaaw" she belted out during an episode of Three's Company was so loud and unexpected that I had tears running down my face from laughing so hard. It sounded like a cross between a chipmunk and a donkey and true to our game, she had to use that laugh the remainder of the show. Each instance sent both of us rolling on the floor, stomachs clenched from laughing so hard. Now I watched television in silence, my stomach clenched a different way, laughter the furthest thing on my mind.

After the fiftieth time going through all 178 channels and zero helpful lessons, I shut off the TV. The stillness that followed reminded me of how alone I really was. I tucked a cushion up into the crook of my armpit and just sat there in a trance. The grandfather clock given to us as a wedding gift finally interrupted the moment I was trapped in and began chiming that it was 10:00 pm. That was the time of night when Vicky would have fallen asleep next to me on the couch, wrapped in a blanket. I could almost feel the weight of her head pressed against my chest as I supported her; insistent upon lying there no matter how many times I shifted. I glanced down, half expecting to see her head, expecting to smell the vanilla extract from the shampoo she used. All I saw was my cushion; there was no one for me to support. I realized that every night would be like this until the inevitable visit from Death. I skimmed the blinking messages to see if I had missed a call from him. No such luck.

Tired of sitting on the couch, I moved to the study and pulled out the notebook. The notebook was intended to hold my handwritten thoughts and feelings, suggested into existence by a certain shrink-in-training on the day of the funeral. Julie had learned in her classes that writing down one's feelings were a therapeutic way to help deal with the pain of a lost loved one. A subconscious release of my emotions would help return me back to normal as quickly as possible, whatever that meant. Normal for me was having a living, breathing wife. But it wasn't like I had anything better to do, so I opened up the notebook to the first page and saw that she had already written in it.

"Always remember, do not waste the precious life

you are given."

As a response I wrote, "How about, don't waste the precious paper in this notebook." and then flipped to the next page, where I began a list of ways to off myself in case I forgot how when the time came.

1. Hang yourself from the shower curtain rod with an electrical cord.

2. Take a bubble bath with a hair dryer.

3. Jump off a building while on fire (in case the fall doesn't do it).

4. Crash your car into a cement wall.

I wrote a few more suggestions, but realized these suicide scenes bored me and promised myself that if I ever did go through with it, I would not use something from this list. I would be spontaneous. Then I went to bed.

Chapter 7

Repetition breeds habit breeds routine. This routine became my therapy. As long as my day-to-day life happened in little packets of time, I dealt with Vicky's death at the appropriate time in the schedule, instead of the full grieving process it probably deserved to be. Wake up, eat breakfast, shower, catch train to work, work, catch train home, eat dinner, watch TV, mourn Vicky, write in notebook, go to sleep, repeat. I concentrated only on getting from one step to the next. If even one detail was out of place, my mind fell off track and I fell apart.

I realized my need to adhere strictly to this schedule last week when I attempted to get from "catch train to work" to "work" and Sheila wasn't on the train. This was my time to visit with my train friends. I frantically looked around but couldn't find her. I became very anxious and the world started closing in on me. Everything was not in its right place. I selfishly thought that she had left me; another person gone from my life. Beads of sweat turned into drops and ran down my face. My stomach tightened into a hard ball and I felt the fist that would soon start squeezing it. My breaths became shallow and rapid; I couldn't get enough air.

"Morning, Frank," Neil said, settling in to his seat.

"How you feeling today?"

"Hey, Neil, I'm doing alright. Much better than Sheila, to say the least," Frank replied over the empty bench between them.

"Oh, yeah? What's the deal with her? Where is she, anyways?"

"Well, she emailed me Friday night about something she ate. Said her stomach had been messed up all day. Asked if I had any Tums or anything I could drop by."

"Oh yeah, I forgot you guys live down the street from each other or somethin', right?"

"Across the street, yeah. Anyway, I didn't have anything in the house, but offered to go to the store and pick something up," Frank said, as Neil nodded along with the story.

Frank continued, "She didn't want anything, so I told her I hoped she felt better. She called me last night to say she'd be taking the day off work, in case we were looking for her."

"Ah, poor gal. Hope she feels better soon. Looks like it's boys ride in, so why don'tcha move on up here. You're not going to believe the shit that happened on my boat this weekend. I swear to god, I saw a shark fin in the water..."

Frank moved up a row into Sheila's regular seat and Neil continued on with his story. The instant Frank told Neil that Sheila was out sick, the pressure lifted from my chest and my breathing returned to normal.

I spent the rest of the ride analyzing what had just happened and my reaction to it. Julie would have called it transference, the redirection of internal feelings about someone to a completely different person. She had warned me something like this might happen. I technically didn't even know these people and almost flipped out because one of them took a sick day. I chalked the whole thing up to the tired overemotional state of my mind. During the last few months that I had existed only in my therapeutic schedule, I had exchanged sleeping for working non-stop, crunching number after number, trying to save the world or make plastic bottle caps for water. The only human contact I had was with my train friends. Like a very powerful machine that overheats from running non-stop for too long, my mind had just overcompensated for my loss of Vicky, making me feel more attached to these people than I really was. I probably just needed to sleep.

But sleep was difficult since Vicky had died. I was afraid to lie down and drift off because of the dreams that would hammer me. The most twisted and disturbing nightmares of my entire life. The first one occurred right after Vicky's funeral.

I was alone in a desert, sitting on top of a hill made completely out of sand. The landscape in every direction was dried out clay; broken chunks of it creating gaping holes in sections of the surface like dried human skin peeled back from a wound. The bottom of a hot pulsating sun had just kissed the flat horizon; foreplay before it actually disappeared into it. This embrace cast a strange glow over everything the remaining rays touched, turning it all into gold for a moment.

I was naked except for shorts, with a wooden staff in my right hand and a rusty six shooter gun in my left. I tried standing up on top of the sand mound, but kept sinking as the sand shifted, sucking me down. The sand and I finally reached a compromise with my legs buried almost up to my knees but still standing. From this height, I saw a thick black shadow begin to coat the earth like molasses as the sun completed its penetration into the earth.

During the final moments of the golden light, an enormous rat burrowed up from a peeled scab in the ground and ran towards me, keeping just ahead of the darkness covering the land. The rat was the size of a small chihuahua dog and had black fur matted down with either grease or dried blood. It bound towards me like a jackrabbit, its two back legs pushing its whole body forward, followed by its two front legs pulling its body. Then I saw that it was blind. Where its eyes should have been, there was nothing but dark gray scarred skin over the sockets. An unnaturally long and deformed tongue hung out of the front of its mouth between rows of sharp, pointy teeth as it panted. The bulbous, bumpy tongue touched the ground, slightly dragged under its legs from the forward motion.

Using what little light remained, I aimed the gun and shot at it with six quick pulls of the trigger. However, instead of bullets, six black and yellow wasps flew stinger first out of the gun like darts into the rat. They stung it to what should have been its death. The sounds emitted from the creature with each sting reminded me of a colicky baby crying for its bottle. Still screeching, its oversized tongue spun around and swatted at its attackers. One after another, the wasps were curled into the oversized pink tongue, crushed, and eaten. Blood poured freely from the sting wounds in the rat's body, legs, and even the scar tissue covering the right eye socket. It stopped for a moment and I was sure it was going to die, but instead it launched itself into the air, aimed straight at me.

I knew that it would kill me if it fell on me, so I threw the empty gun aside and got into a batter's stance with the staff. I prepared to hit the thing as it descended. In a panic, I quickly flashed back to the memory of Vicky's and my first date to the batting cages, where I misjudged a ball and ended up with a broken nose. I wasn't about to let that happen again. I couldn't miss. When the rodent came down, I swung as hard as a lumberjack trying to take down a tree with one swing.

I missed.

The rat didn't.

It hit me squarely in the chest, directly over my heart, its claws sinking into my bare skin. I felt each individual digit of each paw slip into and under my skin, securing its grip on me. I grabbed its bloody, greasy fur and ripped it away from my body. Instantly, four strips of flesh ripped from my chest like Band-Aids and warm blood flowed down my torso. The writhing animal nearly slipped from my grip as it attempted to latch back onto my flesh with swimming motions of all four appendages. Its head craned forward, tongue lapping at the sweat freely dripping down my neck; I could feel its hot breath as it looked for any means possible to attach itself to me.

I threw it to the ground and it landed at my feet, momentarily stunned. I raised the staff over my head with both hands and prepared to bring it down on its head. As I brought it down with all of my force, I saw that the staff had become a human arm, hand attached, both stiff with rigor mortis. I did not complete the swing due to shock, and dropped the arm to the ground, where my instinct took over. I bashed the rat's skull in with my bare heel, stomping on it over and over until the parched ground drank everything that flooded out of its corpse.

Crouching over the lifeless body, I felt the arm grab hold of my ankle. It was trying to claw its way up my leg. Just before the final speck of golden light dotted out of existence and threw everything into complete blackness, something sparkled on the hand wrapped around my calf. It was the engagement ring I had given my wife over nine years ago.

Chapter 8

The Happy Couple was out again for the third consecutive Monday. I could no longer convince myself that they were just on vacation or had finally decided to tie the knot and were on their honeymoon. A vacation takes you away for a week, a honeymoon possibly two. This was week three. I was more paranoid than I was when Sheila took that sick day four weeks ago, my stomach constantly flipping end over end. At least with Sheila, the sickening anxiety only lasted a few moments before I found out that she was just out for the day. With the Happy Couple, I had no idea where they were or when they'd return. Each day last week when they hadn't shown up resulted in a night of my not eating or sleeping. The consistency in my life abandoned me, my pattern was broken, and I realized that I was, too.

With the Happy Couple was gone, a new train acquaintance gave me a temporary solution. I didn't classify him as a friend yet, but the first time I saw him across from me on the upper level of the train, he was drinking out of a flask. He saw me looking at him, and sitting back with his black leather boots perched on the metal rail in front of him, he lifted the flask up to the brim of his black cowboy hat. With a nod of his head and a "here's to you" gesture, he took a swig. He tilted his hat down over half-closed eyes, crossed his arms over his chest, and sat there with a content smile spread across his face. He seemed relaxed and at peace with himself. I envied that.

That same night, as an experiment, I found some Stoli vodka in the basement and filled one of the many flasks I had dutifully collected from standing up in various friends' weddings. I was never much of a drinker, and skeptical that the idea would work in the first place, but I soon found that a few sips while watching TV relaxed me enough to stop worrying about Gina's and Rob's whereabouts. The alcohol also helped me sleep and worked great for a few nights. But a week later, I didn't want to sleep. Because a week later, I dreamed of them.

In my dream, Rob, Gina, and I were on the train like any other normal day. However, when we arrived downtown, for some reason, instead of heading west to my job, I followed them east. Something told me to follow them closely without being seen, so I blended in with the crowd of other pedestrians while remaining close enough to hear. Gina was using her indoor voice to yell at Rob for not feeding the cat.

"But it's your cat," Rob interjected, the smug look on his face suggesting that he had already won the argument.

"Yes, but it's our house, Rob. We share responsibilities and you need to start doing more to help out." This could have been a scene from my life with Vicky. The constant stream of drabble going in one ear, not processing, and then going right out the other. Even in my dream, I wondered if things would have been different had some of Vicky's words actually stuck and if I had paid more attention.

"But I don't want the cat. I'm allergic to cats. If you really wanted to make a life together, wouldn't you get rid of the cat so that I could be happy?"

"You'll learn to deal with him. We can get you medicine or shots to help with your allergies."

"So, basically, I have to change my life to accommodate your cat?"

They went on and on and on, back and forth. It was one of those debates that no one would win until one side accepted change. They still held hands as they walked, so I knew that the argument wasn't too serious.

When they got to the end of the block, they cut through an unfriendly looking alley that contained only graffiti and garbage cans. There were muddy puddles filled with wet garbage placed sporadically on the ground, and the sky somehow seemed darker over this particular section of the street. I thought it was very strange that they would take a shortcut that personified every parent's warning to their kids about cutting through alleys. Not to mention this alley didn't appear to lead anywhere. There was a tall cement wall at the other end.

Gina's cream coat hopped and skipped over the ground as she walked. I could see mud soaking into it every time it touched down. Rob's white rubber soles matched the rest of his black Converse shoes as he walked directly through the sludge. The farther they walked into the alley, the more the color drained away from everything, fading into a black and white photograph, until only the black was left. The sun was gone and it was suddenly night, a dangerous dark gray sky filled with fat purple thunderclouds that threatened a storm. Neither of them noticed as Gina continued to scold him, their steps almost in sync. She had moved on from the cat and now droned on about tracking mud into the house. They almost reached the wall at the end of the alley. The entire time, I saw only their backs. Then, about ten feet from the wall, they stopped and faced each other, nose to nose, still holding hands, Rob hunched over Gina's tilted head. Their faces were so close together I could see the silhouette of a tilted wine glass spilling against the dark backdrop.

Keeping in constant contact, they slowly rotated against each other, foreheads touching, and looked in my direction, seeing me as a movie star sees the camera. Their conversation ceased and they were both possessed zombies, glazed eyes housed in touching heads, tilted at awkward angles.

I wanted to break the silence and ask them why they stopped, but I was cut off when a clothesline shot across the alley. There were no windows in the crumbling brick walls that encased this nightmare diorama, so I had no idea where it came from. The thick rope was simply anchored in the bricks of one side of the wall and disappeared into the other side. Plastic infant dolls spanned the entire length of the clothesline, each hanging from its own little noose. From the motion of the rope, a few dolls were still clicking together in a sadistic Newton's Cradle. In the center of the line were two larger nooses. Rob and Gina stepped towards these and slipped them around each other's necks, tightening the premade knots. They kept their empty gaze upon me and their eyes had gone as pure white as Neil's hair.

Then they spoke one word to me.

"Stanford."

Each took one syllable and repeated it in sequence over and over, speaking in the same monotonous tone. It was not their natural voices. It sounded forced, as if some other source plucked their vocal cords like guitar strings to form each half of the word.

As the vocal symphony repeated endlessly in the background, a jelly-like substance slid out from the closest garbage Dumpster. The only association I could make was that it looked very similar to the shock propaganda the anti-abortion people passed out on the streets. The red bubbly mass gurgled its way over to Rob and Gina, and rose up in the air behind them by transforming into the shadow of a man. There were no distinct features on this new form, just the basic shape of a human coated in all black.

Time slowed down; everything moved at half speed. A shin-length trench coat manifested and wrapped itself tightly around the body. A wide-brimmed hat appeared, still dripping with mucous. The man tilted his head in my direction in a "here's to you" gesture, flicked open a switchblade knife, and without a word, wrapped his left arm around Rob's forehead. Cradling his forehead in the crook of his elbow, he used his other arm to slit Rob's throat. The arm holding his forehead pulled back slightly so that the red-hot blood spurted forward. In less than ten seconds, Seurat's newest painting appeared on Gina's face.

Gina didn't move or even seem to notice. She sat there like the blank canvas she had become. When Rob's neck stopped spurting blood, the shadow man let him go and he hung there from the noose like an unused puppet. The noose caught just under his Adam's apple, slightly pushing the cartilage out of his body, like a turtle peeking its head out of its shell. His lifeless white eyes looked straight into the sky, while the rest of his body just hung there, limp.

The shadow man turned to Gina, whose red face almost blended in perfectly with her hair, and began punching her eye sockets. Still in slow motion, left hand met left eye, right hand met right eye. Left then right, sometimes both at the same time. The noose held her upright, acting as a pendulum to continually swing her back to his fists. He pounded each eye countless times, long enough for each punch to produce a thick wet sound like raw meat dropped on a counter. He paused momentarily and from out of his trench coat he pulled a familiar wooden staff. The staff was an extension of his being, formed to shape from the same black sludge he himself had manifested. It was the same staff I had tried to kill the rat with in my first dream. I shuddered, recalling how it had turned into Vicky's arm right before I woke up. The staff exposed, the man began hitting Gina in the face with broad powerful swings. When he was either done or too tired to continue, he dropped the weapon, which then transformed into a brown and yellow snake that slithered off under a Dumpster. Gina's head looked like a smashed pumpkin on Halloween. Two gaping eye sockets, made even larger from the collapsed bones, stared out into nothing. Her eyeballs had been popped and I could see a twinkle of green trapped in the blob of jelly slowly sliding down her right cheek. I had never seen a caved in skull like that, not even in the movies.

Whether it was out of shock, fear, or just the way things are in dreams, I was frozen where I stood. My legs were like oak trees planted in the ground. Helpless to run, trying to escape the horror directly in front of me, I looked up at the walls and saw that the bricks were bleeding. Dark red blood ran down both walls in streams towards the clothesline. The line soaked up the blood, sucking it from the wall like a straw; the exact amount measured by how far the red stain traveled. As the blood traversed the noose of each doll, the line turned from an object to a living umbilical cord. The dolls started crying and twisting, coming alive one by one as the blood fed them. Writhing and shrieking at the end of their nooses, their faces became as red as Gina's. The walls stopped bleeding just as the two infants farthest in began feeding from the cord. There wasn't enough blood to get to Gina and Rob's lifeless bodies, so they just hung still and dead in the center of the clothesline, surrounded by hanging, choking, dying babies.

While I watched this horror, the shadow man disappeared. Time resumed its normal progression and I was able to move again. More importantly, I was able to scream. And that's what I did until I woke up in a pool of my own sweat.

Chapter 9

It took me until the fourth Monday without the Happy Couple to realize that my flask-drinking acquaintance was the shadow man from my dream. The cowboy had been habitually boarding the morning train with Sheila, Frank, Neil, and me, so I upgraded him to my newest train friend. Unlike my other friends, though, he sat alone on the top level. I had no way to find out his real name through an overheard conversation so I decided to name him myself. I considered a list of possible names.

Tom. Tom Cruise. Tom Hanks. This guy did not

have movie star qualities.

Dick. Dick Cheney. I really wasn't that into politics.

Harry. Harry Caray. I didn't like sports, either.

I named him Shawn. A name I associated with nothing.

Shawn wore the same shin-length trench coat and wide-brimmed hat that I saw in my dream. His black leather boots had silver clasps over each ankle – a real modern-day cowboy. Other than his attire, he had no real distinguishing features and never spoke to anyone. He preferred to sit in the upper level of single seats facing the center, across from me and over my friends. He carried no briefcase, backpack, or even coffee for that matter; nothing that would suggest he was on his way to a regular nine-to-five job, nothing that really attached him to anything.

We shared the hobby of people watching. Hearing any conversation from my friends below, he would crane his neck to get a better listen, to indulge in the joy of being a silent part of an actual relationship. I'd watch him watch my friends and every time he caught me looking at him, he gave me that same tilted head nod I saw in my dream. Each nod seemed to say, "They're our friends now," and would send a twinge of jealousy right through my gut.

With Shawn's presence also came frequent disruptions in the train schedule. I'd been taking the same train to work for close to seven years, since Vicky had encouraged me to suck it up and deal with the long commute if I really wanted the job in the city. It had rarely ever broken down. Shawn had been a regular for just one week when it broke down twice – not including the time that a car accident near the gates knocked a cement wall directly into the path of the train and delayed it for two hours while the scene was cleaned. I couldn't decide if these were just strange coincidences or if they actually meant something. Given my recent dream, and that Rob and Gina were still missing, I began to wonder. And worry.

I got to work late that day, thanks to a stuck door at the third stop of my commute. It wasn't safe to continue travel until the door was shut, so we had to wait for a guy to drive all the way in from the station near my house to fix it. While we waited, Shawn caught my eye and gave me an empathetic shoulder shrug as if to say, "What are you gonna do?" As he tilted his hat down, I thought I saw something else glimmer just behind the surface of his eyes – something devious yet almost playful at the same time. I thought about it during the entire walk from the train to my building, and I could not shake the feeling that Shawn's sudden appearance in my life was not by chance. I tried to come up with a reason why until I was rudely interrupted by my actual job.

Julie was waiting for me at my office door. Lately, it seemed like she was constantly near me, taking an interest in whatever I did, and always with an extra button or two undone. I wondered what her angle was. We had always been close at work, but even before Vicky's passing, things had gotten kind of weird between us. She gave me guilt trips for not walking out to the parking lot with her after work, frowned at me for not eating lunch with her, and berated me for not immediately emailing her back after she sent me something. I think she might have misinterpreted our friendship for something more, so I had been trying to distance myself. I had a wife at home and didn't want Julie to think anything would ever happen between us. I made sure she knew my feelings towards cheating. Cheating was one of the worst things you could do to a person and if that's where Julie was headed with her misinterpretations, I wanted nothing to do with it.

"Hey, there! Stark just emailed us a new equation. Says it needs to be done before we go home tonight."

"Before we go home? Why? What the fuck is it even...?"

"....Even for?" she finished with me, grabbing a lock of her blonde hair. Her face flinched, surprised at my foul language. Consoling me, she said, "I know, it sucks, but that's the job. What are you gonna do?" The more she twirled her hair, the more I could tell she was actually looking forward to working late.

"Yeah, I know. But why is getting it done on this very night so important?" I asked, knowing there was no way she had an answer. When it came to the equations we solved, we were in the same boat, paddling in the same foggy lake.

"Not sure, of course. Just know we... Gotta. Get. It. Done." She hit my desk with every word, mocking Mr.

Stark's words from her last review. She had told me that was his attempt to motivate her before sending her off. Her playful smile indicated that she was looking for a laugh, but I just wasn't in the mood and she could tell.

She sighed and her shoulders dropped. "You know, before... you always tried to stay late, to stay away... well... we always had a great time. Now, you just want to rush home. It's not good to spend so much time alone so soon after. Freud says..."

I filtered her out. She had a point. I used to stay late when I had to but I found myself rushing home these days if I knew she would be around.

"...And that's why you shouldn't be spending so much time by yourself."

"I know, I know. Sorry. Let's meet up as soon as possible to get this done."

"Sounds good. Give me about five minutes." She looked at me for a few more seconds and then went back to her office. I weeded through my inbox for the email with the equation and thought about deleting it, pretending it never existed. But I had a feeling another copy would find its way back to me.

"So, where should we start?" Julie asked, appearing at the door a few minutes later. It looked like she had thrown on a layer of makeup and brushed her hair.

"I don't know, I suppose the beginning. I still can't believe he just drops this on us, with no warning." She rolled her chair a little too close to mine.

"That's why he's The Stork," she said to me with a wink and a smile. "The Stork" is what we started calling Mr. Stark one night when we were working late. Not only for the similarity to his last name, but also his nature to just swoop in and drop off something unexpected at any given time.

"Yeah, you're right; I should have learned to expect this shit by now. Alright, what do we have here?" I asked, pulling up the equation in my email. It was a form of Schrödinger's Equation, mostly used in quantum mechanics.

"What do you think we're solving for, a way to keep cats alive?" she asked, half joking.

"Not sure, but we do know that half of the Dirac Constant needs to be less than the change in particle position times the change in momentum," I said.

"I'm not certain about that. Are you sure we even need to use Planck's Constant for this equation? Can't we convert it to the version with the Hamiltonian Operator? We can then use the Potential to figure out the wave function."

I thought this over in my head. She was right, that would be the easier way. I was the one who usually came up with those types of ideas. I attributed my lapse in cognitive speed to recent events.

"I suppose that would work," I told her and started plugging numbers and variables into the computer. Once we had the basic method we were going to use, the rest was just meticulous data manipulation and verification.

We finally came up with our solution around 9:45 pm. We had worked so late I had to take the last train of the night home, which left the station at 10:00 pm. The extra time spent with Julie on that equation kept my mind occupied long enough to forget about how miserable I had become. But when I boarded the train for the long ride home, every disparaging thought about my desolate life rushed back twofold, almost as if I had to make up for the time I had briefly escaped it.

As I settled into my single seat in the top row, I was surprised to see Shawn in the same car. It couldn't be a coincidence that he was in this same car on the same train this late at night. I thought back to my earlier theory about Shawn's appearance causing the disruptions on the train and further convinced myself that they were not independent events. He was also the one that killed the Happy Couple in my dream. The Happy Couple that had been missing in reality for over a month. He tried to appear like he was sleeping, but I could see the dim halogen lights reflecting off of the white slits of his eyes and knew he was awake. He had on his same black trench coat and hat, but something about him was different. I couldn't put my finger on it, at least not then.

The conductor and the assistant conductor walked through the cars asking everyone for their tickets. Riders usually presented a prepaid ticket and the conductors used a tool similar to a hole punch to mark it. When they got to me, I fumbled around looking for my ticket. I realized that in my hurried scramble to catch the last train of the night, I had left it in my coat which was still at the office. Tired of waiting for me to produce a ticket, the conductors said they would catch me on the way back and left through the dual sliding doors onto another car. Frustrated and pissed off that I had to buy a ticket while a prepaid one sat in my office, I felt Shawn's eyes steady upon me, dissolving some of the anger into embarrassment. I sighed and looked up to meet his eyes. He slid his hat to the back of his head and was now awake – or at least not pretending to sleep. His eyes flickered to the seats in front of me, the seats where Rob and Gina would normally have sat in the morning. After a few moments of staring at the abandoned seats of my missing friends, he nodded towards the door the conductors had exited through and said, "I don't think they're coming back." As he said this, his eyes moved back to the empty seats, indicating the real subject of his observation. He then grabbed the top of his hat and slid it down over his face. Conversation over.

Chapter 10

While melting ice cubes created their own entropy in my drink, I analyzed Shawn's words like an equation that had a solution in it somewhere. "I don't think they're coming back." The combination of being tired and drunk launched me into a state of paranoia. I almost had myself convinced that he had done something to the Happy Couple – not exactly how it had happened in my dream, of course, but something bad nonetheless. I contemplated what to do. I couldn't go to the police without solid evidence. Julie would fly off on some psychobabble tangent if I mentioned it to her. The friends and family from the funeral had been there for Vicky, not me. I had no one else. I grabbed a picture of us from the mantel over the fireplace and spoke directly to it. Through a steady stream of tears, I begged her to help keep me from losing my mind.

I set the picture back on the mantel with the utmost care. It was from a nature hike we had taken though Yosemite Park about seven months before. On a whim, we hopped in the old beaten-up Honda Civic, now browner from rust than the original paint, and just left for the weekend. The story behind the picture was something we had many laughs over. In the middle of all of God's natural wonder, there we were running around looking for a bathroom. There wasn't one on any of the trails we hiked through. The irony had us laughing so hard that the search to find a bathroom was almost no longer needed.

We finally stumbled upon an outhouse and decided that this was one memory we wanted to capture on film. That explained why we were both crossing our legs in the picture. My eyes blurred over with more tears, and the dual image they created showed me every reason I hurt two times.

I lost perspective on the main focus of the picture. There were about fifteen other people in the background flocking to the outhouse like bees to honey, but what stuck out was the man wearing the black Converse shoes. And then it hit me. What I couldn't put my finger on before. Shawn wasn't wearing the black leather boots I had seen him in every day since we became train friends; he had on black Converse sneakers. I don't see how I could have missed that. I used to be good at picking out the minor details.

My knees buckled and my breath grew short. I struggled against the gray that was trying to steal my vision. Rob had worn the same type of shoes and now Rob was gone. Shawn had even acknowledged their absence on the train. In my mind, I knew Shawn had something to do with Rob and Gina, even if it didn't seem possible.

Chapter 11

Shawn and the missing Happy Couple became my new
obsession. As a result, the quality of my life sank even lower.
Over the next few weeks, paranoia crept into every waking
moment and I depended on more and more alcohol to deal
with my life. My wife was gone. And two of my friends had
disappeared. End result: I was still alone. The booze wrapped
my life in a cloudy, vague dream, making everything seem
almost unreal. It was like watching myself in a movie, but
not feeling anything. This was fine by me since every
unexpected, unanticipated sound I heard made my body's

heart race, pumping both blood and fear through its veins. If I heard a branch brush an outside window, it was Vicky's killer coming back to finish me off. The wind blowing leaves across the roof was Shawn coming to silence me for what I knew about Rob and Gina. Unlit rooms outlined the shadows of these men, waiting in doorways for me. My neck hurt from so much twisting around, sure that someone was behind me. I held it together enough to convince Julie that everything was great, but like Sheila's gray hair, the reality of my life was a draining toilet, flushing to nowhere you'd ever want to go.

Alone in the house that was once our home, my routine had switched from frozen dinners and reruns on TV to chilled vodka tonics and reruns of Vicky's death playing over and over in my head, like some scratched DVD stuck on the same snippet of image and sound.

I still couldn't believe it had happened. I had to work late to solve one of the endless math problems, so Vicky was home by herself. I called to tell her I would be home late and to go ahead and eat without me. She told me she would save any leftovers and to take my time, don't rush. She knew how much this job meant to me and that there would be sacrifices on her part when I took it. I should have rushed. What I came home to was worse than any nightmare I've ever had, recent ones included.

I parked next to her car in the garage after driving home from the train station. Right away I knew something was wrong. Vicky had always been a Christmas junkie, putting the tree up before Halloween, setting porcelain snowmen around the house, and hanging lights off of everything that even slightly resembled a hook. She loved it and I loved her, so that was how it went. When I got home that night after another long day at the office, there were no blinking red and green lights shining out from the front window where our tree stood. The rest of the house was also completely dark. I figured that Vicky had fallen asleep on the couch after work and just hadn't turned them on.

I walked into the house without making a sound so I wouldn't disturb her and looked at the couch. She wasn't there. I thought that maybe she was upstairs in the bathroom or had gone to bed early. I flipped on the foyer lights and made my way to the kitchen, planning to grab a bag of Doritos and bottle of Pepsi, check on Vicky, and then watch some TV. When I grasped the light switch in the kitchen before turning it on, it felt slick, the way your hands feel after putting moisturizing lotion on them. The switch flipped up, the lights came on, and my life changed forever.

On her stomach, head turned to face the heat register beneath the row of cabinets, was my Vicky. She was dead. The plastic Ziploc bag pulled tightly over her head was not expanding or contracting with her breath. The once translucent bag was splattered red, like someone had beaten a tomato inside of it. Her arms were stretched out, both palms faced up towards the ceiling, and each hand had been nailed to the floor. A horizontal crucifixion. I stepped forward right into the puddle of warm blood dribbling out of the bag. The brushed silver handle jutting out from the side of her neck belonged to the knife we had cut our wedding cake with so many years ago. What began our life together had now ended it. I barely made it to the bathroom before I threw up. Then I just sat on the cold tile floor, one arm resting on the toilet, the other one hanging uselessly on the floor next to me. I stared into nothing and entered a state of shock. When I discovered my vocal cords, the sounds emitted from my body couldn't be described as screams. They were inhuman noises thrust out from the very depths of my being. This went on until I slumped over onto the toilet and passed out.

The police later told me that the actual cause of death had been a blow to the head by a blunt object, possibly a bat. That was supposed to make it easier on me, knowing that she wasn't subjected to such hideous torture prior to her death. Cops were so understanding. They said that the bag and knife business had been done afterward. "Postmortem" was the word they used. They believed that the killer had been in the process of decapitating her when I came home and scared off him or her. They said they didn't understand the nailing her hands to the floor, but that they were working on it.

That's the memory that I've dealt with every night since it happened. My dead wife, nearly beheaded and stuck to the floor like a bug in a box. Her blood soaking through my sock, forcing me to physically touch what was my new reality; an existence filled only with hate, self-loathing, and paranoia, with the bottle my only escape from a constant state of pain and suffering.

Chapter 12

My life existed in a drunken, depressed state for an indiscriminate amount of time. The only indication between being drunk and sober was the pain in my head. If it was throbbing, I needed to drink more. That logic didn't work with the pain in my heart, but it also didn't stop me from trying. I could barely find a glass to drink from. They were scattered everywhere about the house, with sticky film coating the edges and marking the exact spot where I had finished the drink. My journal became full of thoughts and ideas that I hardly remembered writing. Gibberish I couldn't even decipher in the mornings.

"Fuck every with your wife life knife."

"Kill you and morning. You want this."

"Buy drink vodka."

"He killed Rob and Gina."

"Julie is a psycho logist."

"Stop trying. Give up."

"Your Alone."

Friends and family stopped all communication the second they left the reception. The list of things I cared about dwindled to just thoughts of Vicky and my train friends. That list purposefully excluded me.

"You guys will not believe what happened to me this weekend." It had to have been some Monday, and Neil had obviously prepared another extravagant boating story. "I'm out sailing, looking for a good spot to catch some carp and these fucking college guys start circling me on them goddamn wave runners."

"You tell them they were scaring the fish?" Frank offered, helping the story along.

"You're goddamn right I did! I said, 'Hey you douche bags, why don't you quit splashing each other like a bunch of homo mermaids and get the hell outta here?'" Neil said, glancing over at Sheila to make sure he didn't offend her. "Sorry, Frank, nuttin' against your type," he added as an afterthought, winking at Sheila with a grin.

Frank smiled and shook his head, preparing his response to Neil's comment. "Real funny, Neil. You're hilarious. But you know us mermaids don't like being called homos."

Sheila laughed at Frank's response, not hiding the snort that came out with the laugh.

"Well, if you're a mermaid, it's weird that you would even be associated with something that smelled like fish."

"You watch your language in front of the lady," Frank jokingly scolded as he mimed fish gills on his face with his open flapping palms.

"Yeah, yeah, you're right," Neil laughed.

"You know, I'm not so sheltered that I haven't heard things like that before, Neil. I am a big girl," she said between bites of hash brown. Her face reddened and she hoped Neil didn't realize the "big girl" comment could have meant two different things.

"Okay, okay," Neil continued. "Still, I should turn down the potty mouth around the ladies. It's just this damn marina they're putting in is bringing all the inexperienced moron sailors to the area. A bunch of clueless idiots."

It went on like this for the duration of the commute. There was something very therapeutic to me about these unimportant conversations centered around nothing. When I heard them, a sense of normalcy kept my mind off of the real, more disturbing parts of my life. For a few hours a day, it was like I was a part of a group that just sat and talked and laughed. Only I never really talked and I have never laughed. I just sat.

This temporary escape was working well until I started to see Shawn on the train more frequently. He'd been sitting on the bottom row now, closer to my remaining friends, trying to become a part of their group. I got the paranoid feeling that he was planning to do something bad to one or all of them, just like the Happy Couple. And after the dream I had, my feeling became a certainty.

In my dream, I was riding the train with Neil and Frank, just like any other morning. The three of us exited the train at the regular stop, Neil clamoring on and on to Frank about another fantastic boating adventure. I followed closely behind them, but as in real life, they didn't know I was there. For some unknown reason, they started following the tracks of the train we had just exited, walking back towards the direction we came from. Neil balanced himself on one rail like a tightrope walker, while Frank jumped forward in the middle, making sure each foot touched the log of wood that completed the "H" between each rail. Left foot, one log, right foot, next log. This went on for miles in distance, but minutes in dream time. I glanced around after a while and noticed that we were in the middle of a forest. We had walked so far that we were equally as far from nothing in both directions. At this point Neil stopped and looked at Frank.

"Psst. Hey, Frank. You want to see where I keep my boat?" Neil looked around to make sure no one had heard him.

"Yeah, I want to check your bad boy out."

"You're damn right you do!" Neil said, his voice going from loud to soft. "But you have to be very, very quiet."

"Why?" asked Frank with a smile. "Are we hunting wabbits?" Always able to make a joke in the right place.

"C'mon, let's go," said Neil, and he suddenly sprinted away from the train tracks towards the forest.

Frank followed him like a dog to its master, the two of them looking like school boys, racing each other to the tree line, dodging holes and hurdling old stumps. I too made my way behind them, hovering over the ground rather than walking on it. This is the way I sometimes moved in my dreams, with the scenery moving past me while I stayed in one place. I wasn't worried about getting separated when they disappeared into the trees since I somehow felt attached to them as if by an invisible rope.

Suddenly a gigantic lake presented itself, so big that the other side of it couldn't be seen from where I stood. The curved border encompassing the lake both to my left and right was a solid wall of trees. A sea of green surrounding a lake of blue. Similar to the scene with the Happy Couple entering the alley, once I crossed the lines of trees on the edge of the forest, the sky turned a dark, dangerous gray. I looked up, expecting a sudden cloud cover. There were no clouds. It was as if we were in a fishbowl that some giant had draped a scarf over. As the grayness settled in and my eyes adjusted, I found I was able to see the things around me in greater detail. Each individual blade of grass had such clarity, I could have been seeing it through a magnifying glass. The surface of each pebble on the hard packed dirt told me its story of how it had come to be that shape.

Looking down towards the lake, I found Frank and Neil. Neil's college football ring sparkled, reflecting light that was not there. I floated to where they were, not sure if they could see me or not, and hid behind a little wooden shack that faced the long, narrow pier where the two men stood. The shack looked like it hadn't been touched in decades. Dry, rotting wood was in desperate need of treatment. The window and door frames were sporadically cracked, the paint so terribly chipped in some places that I wondered if they ever had been painted in the first place. Through one of the grime-filled windows, past ancient spider webs, I saw a dirt floor surrounded by old paint cans and tarps. In the middle of the floor was a square outline of what looked like a wooden trap door. Fishing and boating supplies were strewn about uneven wooden shelves hanging off of the wall.

"You really gonna take me out on your boat, Neil?"

"I brought you here, didn't I? But you have to do exactly as I say. People that ain't never been on a boat are more likely to hurt themselves just by lack of experience more than anything else."

"Aye aye, Cap'n."

"Tell me, you get seasick?"

"I have no idea, Neil," Frank gulped. "I used to do okay at water parks as a kid."

"Well, we'll just have to see, that's not really the same thing. Just let me know if you're going to yak."

"Um... sure thing."

"Okay, let's go."

They made their way down the narrow pier in a single-file line, Frank following Neil. Their footsteps were in sync, their shoes making simultaneous clomping noises on the dry, warped wood of the pier like tap dancers leaving the stage after a performance. Then the footsteps stopped. I chanced a look from my hiding spot. They were gone. The logical assumption was that they had simply walked off the edge of the pier into the water, except I hadn't heard a splash.

I came out from behind the shack and ran down the pier to have a look. I peered down into the water, which was very still and very black. Further out in the distance, shark fins bobbed to the surface like basketballs suddenly let go after being held underwater. They popped up randomly, swarming in crisscross patterns at speeds that were unnaturally fast. I attributed it to being part of a dream. Thick purple clouds reflected back at me from the cold black water. But when I looked to the sky, there were still no clouds. Keeping an eye out for sharks fins, I dipped my hand into the lake which felt more like oil than water. When I lifted my hand out of the lake there was no runoff; viscous mucus stuck to my fingers.

As I wiped the sticky substance off of my hand, a huge boat floated into my line of vision. It appeared out of nowhere and moved away from the pier towards the middle of the lake. Frank and Neil stood talking at the bow as it passed me. Acting purely on an impulse, I backed up a few steps and took a running leap off of the edge of the pier. Midair, I noticed shark fins circling directly beneath me, waiting. I landed on the boat's stern in one piece, but not without some trouble. When I hit the deck, the forward momentum sent me rolling into a trough of chum. The trough didn't tip over, but the impact was hard enough to thrust a whole slew of bloody fish innards out of the bin. I looked to the bow to see if I was caught. Neil was watching Frank pretend he was the king of the world, which I'm sure everyone does their first time on a boat, and they didn't hear the wet smack of guts slapping the deck. Frozen in anticipation to see if I would be discovered, I saw something move out of the corner of my eye. The misplaced heap of stinking skin and organs jiggled like a Jell-O mold and began to take shape: the familiar shape of a man in a hat and trench coat the same color as the thick disgusting water through which we were sailing.

I rolled under a pile of fishing nets near the side of

the boat in an attempt to hide and positioned myself so I could see the entire rear deck in addition to the remaining forty or so feet of the boat's starboard side. Neil descended into the cabin below deck and I watched the newest member of the crew creep towards Frank, his black Converse shoes squishing and sliding through fish guts. Frank still faced the direction of the boat's travel, arms spread out to hug the wind that held down what hair he still had left on the sides of his head. Although I only saw the back of him, in my mind I could see his eyes closed with a smile on his face, the deep worry lines causing the air to stream past him in all directions. Shawn looked towards the pile of nets I was under, gave me that awful nod I'd grown to hate, and slowly walked towards the front of the boat. It was obvious he knew I was there and wanted me to see what was about to happen. I tried to scream out a warning, but the nature of the dream kept me frozen where I was.

Time slowed down and Shawn made his way to where Frank stood unaware. Along the way, he grabbed an emergency axe and the metal pole used to save drowning passengers from the side of the boat. The instant Shawn's filthy hands made contact with the pole, it turned into a brown and yellow snake. He whispered something to the snake and it went rigid. In one fluid motion, he heaved it at Frank like a javelin. The snake kept its stiff form as it flew straight through the air until it hit Frank in the back of the head. Upon impact, it turned into the wooden staff I'd seen in my other dreams. The staff entered the rear of Frank's skull with a crisp sound, like twisting a head of lettuce in half. The next sound I heard was like a sopping wet paper towel thrown against a cabinet, created as a hunk of brain exited the hole in Frank's forehead and slapped against the inner wall of the boat. The staff was held perfectly parallel to the boat's deck, visible in its entirety except for what was hidden inside Frank's mind. The split second before gravity took over seemed to last for minutes. Frank appeared to be hanging from the staff, instead of him holding it up. Momentum finally ended the moment and he fell forward. The wooden staff hit the deck and stuck straight up in the air, held in place like a tripod with Frank's two legs. Gravity called to the blood in his brain and when enough lubrication coated the staff, Frank slowly slid down it onto his face.

Shawn ran up behind Frank with the fire axe and I shut my eyes. All I heard was chopping, scraping, and clanking as Shawn made Frank into more chum.

I opened my eyes, determined to get off of that boat. No longer worried about the sharks waiting for me, I fled from the nets and jumped overboard into the thick black water. I expected the worst but the sharks were all dead and floating in the water, their soulless black eyes open, just not seeing me. I swam as fast as I could through the thick goo back to the pier. Scrambling out of the water, exhausted and out of breath, I turned around to look at the boat. I saw that it had turned starboard, with the entire length of the side now facing the pier. The boat's name, Stanford, was painted in black letters towards the front. Right above the name was Frank's head, impaled on a decorative bow made of the wooden staff, bobbing up and down with the gentle waves of the lake. He always nodded at just the right places.

Chapter 13

I only registered that I had mistakenly poured orange juice into my cereal instead of milk when I piled the dishes onto the ever-rising heap on the counter and saw pulp at the bottom of the bowl. I didn't care. My head was pounding; I was too hung-over. For three days after that dream, I'd been drinking enough so I wouldn't dream at all when I passed out. That was how I got by. Between Vicky's death, my dreams, and missing friends, it was all I could do. I calculated that a fifth of vodka bought me about three solid hours of heavy sleep. Two fifths and I'd be dead. Being a

Numbers Analyst, I was able to find the average of the two.

Frank had not been on the train since that dream. The paranoia that accompanied my nightly drinking binges made me confident that Shawn had something to do with the disappearance of both him and the Happy Couple. I watched Shawn watch Neil and Sheila, absorbing everything they said. I could tell that they felt something was wrong, too. Their voices were merely a whisper and they both sounded worried.

"Hey, Sheila, you talk to Frank over the weekend?" Neil tried to sound casual, like he was just passing time, but his voice wavered past the frown he tried to hide.

"Nope. I was hoping you had. Think he's sick or somethin'?"

"Don't know. He was supposed to come check out my boat over the weekend, but he never showed up and never called, either. A guy like Frank wouldn't fuck me over like that for no reason. He's usually good for his word. You sure you ain't heard nuttin'?"

"I can try emailing him when I get to work. I haven't seen him outside these past few days," she said. The greasy wrapper crumpled around the rest of her breakfast burrito as she squeezed it. "You don't think something happened, do you?" Her eyes widened with worry and she shoved the rest of her burrito in the bag. She seemed to have lost her appetite. I swore I caught just a glimpse of a smile from under that dark brim of Shawn's hat.

"Nah, probably just sick like you said... I would think." During that miniscule pause, Neil looked past Sheila to Shawn and decided against saying something more before continuing with a shrug. "Just email him and let me know."

If those two were so worried about Frank, I was a fucking mess. I digressed to the point where I just stumbled into work late and collapsed hung-over into my chair. The wrinkled noses of people that passed by and the secret whispers outside of my office walls were as obvious as the reasons for them in the first place. I wasn't trying to hide anything, but I made a mental note to use more cologne to cover the smell of Stoli. But cologne wouldn't do much to improve my ever-suffering work. Yesterday my vision had been so blurred that a "1" became a "77" and I messed up an entire equation. I could have killed millions, but more than likely just made the font bigger on a candy bar wrapper somewhere.

Nights continued to be the loneliest time for me. If I wasn't thinking about how to deal with Shawn, I was thinking about her. My wife. My one and only truly best friend in this god-for-fucking earth. Taken from me by some fucking psychopath that was still out there somewhere, going about his day-to-day business. Go to work, come home, kill someone, eat dinner, repeat. We all had our routines. If I ever found this guy, I would kill him, I swear I would. He had taken my Vicky before she was supposed to go and I wanted to take from him what he had taken from me – everything.

The little things were the hardest to get over. These miniscule details that meant absolutely nothing at the time were the grains of salt sprinkled into a huge open gash in my heart. No one yelled at me for squeezing the toothpaste from the middle instead of the end of the tube. No one folded my socks into a ball instead of in a knot because it didn't stretch them. No one scratched my arm from the elbow all the way to the palm in the middle of the night. There was no one. I was in a fucking mess of a house, itching, with socks hanging off of my feet, and a whole fuckload of toothpaste at the bottom of the tube. I was a disaster, I knew it. My co-workers knew it. Fuck, even my imaginary friends on the goddamn train probably knew it. And I didn't care. I gave up.

It was another night sometime in my life. I had my head down hoping that the ceiling would fall in on me. Hoping that by some miraculous sequence of events, a meteor would fall through my roof and just end this all for me. I opened my notebook to jot down these new ideas and saw the original advice that Julie had written in there: "Always remember, do not waste the precious life you are given." What a fucking joke, I thought to myself, and just to stress how much I meant this, I said it out loud.

"What a fucking joke."

It was at that point, at that very moment in time, that I became fully aware that I was wasting my life in the catacomb of my own mind, surrounded by the memories of my dead wife and my dead or dying friends. Dead or dying friends that I was doing nothing about. That I was just letting slip out of my life. Dead or dying friends that most likely had families or loved ones of their own, like Vicky was to me. It suddenly dawned on me that I needed to stop Shawn. I had already accepted my life as a waste, but if I was able to save others from the pain I was going through, perhaps I could get some feeling of closure in losing Vicky. Logical thinking told me that I would need more proof than just a few dreams and new shoes. I needed to study Shawn and see what he was up to after our time together on the train ended. For the first time since Vicky's death, I was beginning to feel like I might still have a purpose.

Chapter 14

The next day I called off work. I planned to follow Shawn after the train ride to learn as much as I could about him. I gave The Stork some shit excuse about needing to catch up on much-needed sleep. Given my almost immediate return to work after Vicky died, he had no objections. He told me to take all the time I needed, not worry about anything at the office, and to call him if I needed anything. As I hung up the phone, I wondered if he had read that line from the manager's training manual or if he had actually committed it to memory.

Despite not having to go to work, I still got on the train at my regular time, hoping to run into Shawn. As the doors parted and I entered into my tin can of choice, I discovered I wasn't the only one that missed my friends.

"Hey, Neil, I emailed Frank but he never emailed me back. You ever hear from him?" asked Sheila. I walked up the narrow steps to the single seats and saw that her appetite had regressed even more, noted by the lack of items pushing out the sides of a greasy bag.

"Nope, nuttin' yet. He's gotta be sick or on vacation or somethin'," Neil said, staring off into nothing. His tone was monotonous and it seemed like he was trying to convince himself as well as Sheila.

"Yeah, maybe he just forgot to tell us." Her mouth turned into a pouting frown. "You remember when you spent a whole week at that marina protest last year? We didn't know until after it was over."

"How could I forget? You gave me so much shit for not telling you. Not that it mattered one goddamn bit. They're still building the fucking thing. Maybe Frank's at some mermaid march?" They tried to remain positive for each other, but their drooping shoulders and wandering gazes indicated that they both thought something was wrong. They just refused to admit it.

Right before the main doors closed, my remaining friend boarded the train. Shawn looked at all of us through the window in one of the doors to our car before he opened them. He stood there with the doors fully open for a few moments and then slowly made his way down the aisle, looking for a place to sit. Sheila and Neil's eyes dropped to avoid looking at him. Shawn took his seat five rows back and sat facing them, staring.

I had told myself last night that I was going to watch this son of a bitch every minute of the commute, so I did. He had on his same trench coat, hat, and Converse shoes. I attempted to study his face so I could identify him in a police lineup when I got my proof, but it was difficult with his hat on and the steep angle from where I sat viewing him. I could only see his clean-shaven jaw and thin lips pressed together in no particular shape. And that was it, that was all I could see. For the entire commute, he just sat facing Neil and Sheila, expressionless.

As for my plan to follow Shawn and see where he went, I never got my chance. Sometime after the fifth stop, a long screech followed by a large clunk interrupted the ride. It sounded like whatever caused the clunk had been run over as we slid to a halt. Something had detached itself from the train and the abrupt jolt rocked the car from side to side. Sheila and Neil stopped their conversation and, like most of the other passengers, looked around for an explanation. Shawn however, just sat there unmoving, as if he had expected this.

"What the fuck was that?" Neil asked to no one in particular. The train came alive with theories as to what had happened.

"Did the brake system lock up?" asked a woman I didn't know.

"Did we hit something?" asked an old lady with far too many bags for one bench.

"No way, we would have heard a thud or something. This was metal scraping more metal."

"Terrorists?"

"Aliens?"

"The end of the world?" The seconds clicked off and the ideas got more ridiculous. It's amazing what the mind made you think when there was no one around to tell you what was going on.

"It was just its time to break," offered Shawn, showing signs of life for the first time during the entire trip. The other suggestions had all been questions. Shawn's comment was a statement, spoken like he already knew the answer.

A minute later a voice came over the loudspeaker. "Ladies and gentlemen, we're sorry to inform you that the train has experienced a mechanical malfunction and will temporarily be out of service."

The collective groan harmonized around the same tone.

"We realize that this is a great inconvenience to you all and we're trying to come up with alternate solutions. We have no exact time estimate on how long the repairs will take, but we're guessing around an hour or two. In the meantime, we have flagged down the train behind us, rerouted it to the opposite rail, and asked it to stop and pick up any passengers from this train. You can either sit it out on this train, or carefully cross the tracks to the other side and squeeze in with them."

The obvious choice was to get on the other train. Everyone stood up and tried leaving the train at once, which only caused the process to take much longer. I technically didn't have anywhere to go, so I decided to do whatever Shawn did. But somewhere in the sea of sardines trying to escape through the bottleneck, I lost him. He must have slipped out before everyone else, most likely because he had known this was going to happen. Without Shawn, I was in no rush to board another train by any given time, so I decided to stick it out on my current train. After a quick discussion with myself, I decided that 7:30 a.m. wasn't too early to start drinking and pulled out my flask. A single flask was not enough to drop me into that deep dreamless sleep I longed for, but it was enough to put me to sleep. So I slept. And I dreamt.

Chapter 15

In my dream, the train was deserted, empty except for
Sheila, Neil, and me. I began to panic. I knew where this was
headed and I wanted to stop it before it started. Sheila
looked around from left to right as if she had just woken up
without a clue that she was on a train in the first place. I
looked around from left to right and saw we were
surrounded by white. Outside, everything everywhere was
white. Snow covered the ground as far as the eye could see
and there was not a building, a tree, or even a twig
anywhere. It was as if a giant artist had placed the train in

the middle of a blank canvas; we were all that existed because the world around us hadn't been created yet. Sheila got up to exit the train.

"Where are..." I started to ask, trying to make contact with her, with either of them. I stood up but was pushed back into my seat by an unseen force. My voice was torn from me like a syringe ripped from an addict's arm. Something wanted me to observe, not to take part.

"There's got to be a place with a phone around here somewhere," she said to Neil.

"Look around us, sweetheart. There's nothing there. I say we stay on the train."

"Well, I have to get out of here. I'm scared. And I don't think it's safe on this train anymore." Her eyes flickered up to the top rows where I sat as she spoke. Looking back to Neil, she said, "Come with me." Without waiting for a reply, she made her way towards the door. I looked through my glass window and saw that her footprints sank deeply into the snow as she walked. She wasn't moving fast, pulling each foot up and over the snow before thrusting it forward to take the next step.

I looked down at Neil. He sat, arms crossed, rubbing his triceps. He closed his eyes and let out an audible sigh. He said, to no one in particular, "I warned her." Then he dozed off. I got up and exited the train.

I followed the deep holes Sheila had made in the sea of white like a connect-the-dots puzzle. A few feet away from the train, I turned around and noticed I was not making any footprints. I turned back and saw Sheila tromping up ahead towards more whiteness. She still grasped the greasy bag of fast food in her right hand, and it swung forward in a wide arc with each struggling step, her left hand swinging back for balance.

It began to snow. The sharp little flakes plummeted down like hail, stinging my skin and obfuscating everything. The once contrasting image of white ground against a gray horizon was now just a solid block of white, as pure as Neil's hair. It became difficult to follow Sheila with the hundreds of tiny cold daggers stabbing me from above, cutting both my visibility and my face. I slowly made my way forward by bending over to sweep the snow in front of me with my hand, as if I was looking for mines. Any pit in the snow would be an indication of a recent step.

I continued on this way until my outstretched hands connected with what felt like stone. Hard crusted ice ran the entire length of an upside-down parabola, a frown in the middle of nowhere. The entrance to the cave was the first three-dimensional object I had seen out in this white field. I walked slightly hunched over into the mouth of the cave and the blinding snow stopped stabbing my face. The wall of solid white behind me gave no indication as to how far I had walked.

The mouth of the cave was solid rock, slimy and wet to the touch, and smelled as musty as an opened catacomb after years of decay. As I felt my way deeper inside, shadows danced on the walls, projected by a flickering light from up ahead. Between the shadows, pictures had been drawn on the wall depicting the sacrifice of a small child. I didn't want to know what was used for ink. In the first picture, two figures forcibly carried a smaller figure to a fire surrounded by an audience. In the next picture, remnants of the smaller figure laid smoldering in the fire, while the remaining figures sat around the fire eating. Two-dimensional life lessons from a different time, minus the laugh track.

I felt my way farther back into the cave until it opened up to an enormous domed room. I was in a stone igloo. The ceiling was spiked with stalactites, threatening to pierce anyone unlucky enough to be underneath if one should happen to fall. In the middle of the room, Sheila sat Indian-style in front of the small fire that provided the only available light. She stared into the fire like a woman possessed, pretty eyes unblinking, hypnotized by the dancing flames.

"I'm so hungry and so cold," she said to the fire, as if it was listening to her. The steady tone in her voice enhanced the hypnotic look in her eyes. The rippling waves of light made the shadow of her body dance between the stone spikes overhead. She reached into the greasy bag at her side and gorged on hash browns and Egg McMuffins. She never looked up from the fire as she consumed mouthful after mouthful of food. When she finished, she fed the bag to the fire, which flared up once it lapped up the grease. Burning to nothing, the bag emitted black smoke that rose straight up into the air. But the smoke did not disperse. It stayed concentrated in one mass, and that mass started to take shape. I could make out a thin brim of a hat in the haze. The smoke was becoming Shawn. I tried to scream out a warning, but my voice and body were frozen in place. I was forced to watch, helpless to do anything.

The smoke hovered by her head as if it were whispering to her. She nodded in her trance, not quite hearing, but definitely understanding. She untied her shoes and slipped them off. Her socks came off next. She folded them into a tight ball and pushed them down into her left shoe. She sat barefoot on the floor of packed snow, her eyes never losing contact with the fire. Her breathing quickened to the point that she was almost grunting, and then with one last inhale she stopped. She paused for just a moment, exhaled forcibly, and stuck her right foot into the fire. There was no expression of pain on her face while she sat watching the flames first lick her foot and then engulf it. Her eyes widened in pleasure and a smile crept across her face. The skin of her foot blistered, bubbled, and then turned black. Moments later, hunks of charred flesh slid off her foot into the fire and disappeared with a sizzle, leaving only the muscle and bone underneath. The smell was sickening, greasy fried chicken mixed with a twinge of sweet barbeque. I got a dry, gagging feeling in the back of my throat.

When Sheila felt that her right foot had had enough, she took it out of the fire and placed it on the snow. What remained of her smoldering ruined appendage sank down into the frozen ground, creating steam. She rocked slightly back and brought the charred foot to her mouth, biting into what remained of the arch between the ball and heel. Her eyes flickered back into the fire as she tore out a chunk of cooked meat with her teeth and chewed it. Through a mouth full of herself, she garbled the word "Stanford" as coagulated blood dribbled down her chin.

I still couldn't move, but I had to look away so I concentrated my focus on Shawn. He was no longer black smoke, he had become a man, or at least a solid form that looked like a man. Looking up from Sheila, his eyes met mine, daring me to do something, but knowing damn well that I couldn't do anything. He gave me a slight nod and the entire cave started shaking. Sheila just sat there staring into the fire and chewing, unaware that anything else was going on. The sharp rocks started falling down from the ceiling all around us. Some spikes stuck into the ground where they fell, while others exploded into pebbles and dust upon impact. Shawn smiled. More and more spikes fell, faster and faster. More and more dust built up in the cave, making it harder to see through the already smoky haze. Sheila put her other foot into the fire. As she did this, Shawn plucked an unbroken spike from the floor and walked up behind her.

The stone spear exited her face just under the right eye. A jagged imperfection on the spike jutted up just enough to pierce her kind, green eye and force it out. The momentum caused her torso to follow her eye face-first into the fire, pinning it there as the tip of the stalactite stuck into the red glowing coals. Her single eye sat independent of her body for just a moment before popping like an overheated bean in a microwaved bowl of chili. The smell of burnt hair added to the stench of cooked human meat. Skin from her face, neck, and chest melted off into the fire, hitting the coals with the sound of frying bacon. There were no screams. I hoped to god that she was dead from the initial blow and not from the fire eating her.

"Still haven't figured it out?" Shawn asked me directly. His hand was still wrapped around the other end of the spike sticking out of Sheila's head, like a hiker on a nature trail. Instead of a stone stalactite, I saw that it was the wooden staff. Figured what out? I thought.

Sheila was still cooking in the fire when I was finally able to move again. I tried to run out of there as fast as I could, but visibility was so poor from the smoke and dust that I ran face-first into a wall. I saw stars and dropped to the ground, barely maintaining consciousness. Under the layer of thick black smoke filling the cave, I saw that Sheila's chest was nothing more than an empty cavity of ribs as her smoldering intestines slid out into the fire, like sausages off of a grill.

Chapter 16

I was awakened by a loud clanking sound. The conductor
was banging his ticket-puncher against the metal railing.
"End of the line, buddy!" he yelled, and I couldn't have
agreed more. "You gotta get off here," he continued. While I
was asleep, they had apparently fixed the train and I was now
in the city. No one else was on the train.

"Why'd you stay on the train, pal? Don't you gotta be
anywhere today?" he asked. I told him I was a heavy sleeper
and missed the announcement. I exited the train, silently
answering the second part of his question: I didn't have

anywhere to be. My plan to follow Shawn had failed miserably and I wasted an entire day calling in sick to work. I walked to the nearest liquor store and bought a fifth of Ketel One vodka. They were out of Stoli, but I didn't really care. I walked around the city and thought more about Sheila and my dream. I could only assume that she was gone now, too. I had to figure out what to do about the murderous fuck that was killing my friends.

I sat down on a park bench overlooking the lake and twisted the cap off of my bottle. I attempted to think logically about the situation. Sip. My friends no longer showed up on a train they'd consistently taken for as long as I could remember. Sip. They went missing after I had atrocious dreams about them being murdered. Sip. In each dream, the same person had done the killing. Sip. That person was Shawn. Sip. Even in waking moments, he taunted me with remnants from these murders. His words: "They're not coming back." The Converse shoes. The last thing he asked me: "Still haven't figured it out?" Sip, sip, sip. What did that mean? What was I supposed to figure out? I couldn't make a connection. Dreams, murder, looking, searching, thinking, drinking, paranoia, alone, dead, Vicky, suicide, notebook, reaching out, arm reaching out.

In the first dream I had in the desert, Vicky's arm had reached out and grabbed my ankle. I had been frightened at the time of the dream, but maybe it was a sign, like the one I had asked her for when I held our picture at the park. Her arm had transformed from the wooden staff I used to try to kill that hideous rat; the same wooden staff had appeared in every dream since. I didn't associate the dream after Vicky's funeral with the more recent dreams about my friends, but the wooden staff did seem to be a link between them. I analyzed this in my head for a few minutes. If the wooden staff from my first dream was Vicky's way of reaching out to me from beyond, could it also be a message sent in the dreams about the deaths of my train friends? Shawn had used that wooden staff to kill my friends in each dream. Maybe it wasn't only used to kill my train friends; maybe it had also been used to kill Vicky.

It fit. It felt right. I paused at this revelation, surprised at how calm I was. I think on some level I had always known I would come to the conclusion that Shawn was the one responsible for all of this. Responsible for killing not only my friends but also my wife. Responsible for all of my pain, all of my misery in its entirety. I stood up to breathe in the lake air and clear my head a bit and realized how drunk I had gotten just sitting there on the bench. The skyline appeared to move on its own. I sat back down and looked at my watch. It was barely noon. I lifted the bottle up to my eyes and saw the lake through it, half blurry, half clear. That meant I had half a bottle left. I decided to go get something to eat.

Stumbling through the city, I got completely turned around and lost. I walked aimlessly for about five more blocks before I finally stopped to get a gyro from some place I had never seen before and will never see again. I was in an unfamiliar part of the city and my immediate goal after eating was to get back to the train station and go home. People on the street stared at me like I had just slapped their mothers. I would have been more intimidated if I hadn't been full of liquid courage. About a third of my bottle remained and I wanted to save it for the ride home.

At some corner, I tried asking directions from what

looked to be a Hispanic mother of three watching her kids play near a sewer. She wore a torn button-down shirt opened enough to reveal a sweat stained white t-shirt underneath. Tight neon green Spandex shorts clung to her body making her look like an overstuffed bag of marshmallows. She sat on the corner in a cheap vinyl lawn chair, smoking from a half-empty pack of Marlboro Reds.

"Where's tha..," I paused to catch myself from stumbling over the curb into her chair. I tried again. "Where's tha train stay shun?" I blurted at her, slurring my separated syllables.

"Watch you talk about, mista?" she asked in a heavy accent.

"I need t' get... to catch my train." I put a fist to my mouth, muffling a belch that tasted like vodka mixed with stomach acid.

"You gimme twenty bucks. I tell you."

I cocked my head at her. "You kidding me? I jus' need some fuggin' direc shuns, lady." My voice was leaving my mouth in slow motion. I swiveled my head from left and right, looking around for anyone else to help. I saw no one.

The street had become void of all people and the bright day had rapidly clouded over. Time had slipped away from me again.

"No one here to help you, chico. Gimme twenty bucks and I show you where da train is," she said. I saw from her bloodshot eyes that the money would mean she could get high tonight.

I was getting pissed off. "Screw thish shit, lady, screw't," I said, throwing up my arms to shoo her away. I turned to leave. I'd find the train on my own. It couldn't have been that hard, I'd just retrace my steps. Once I'd remembered them.

"What you say to me, mutha fucka?" She stood up and turned to her kids. "Juan, take your hermanos to the casa, por favor, 'kay? Mommy'll be there in un momento." The seriousness of her tone indicated that something bad was about to happen. The kids whispered to each other, then took off running down the street, giggling at whatever joke they just made.

I wanted this to end before it started. "Listen, miss. I'm tired. N' drunk. I jus' want to go to mi casa, comprendes? So sorry if I....."

"Shut the fuck up, mista. You ain't going shit anywhere without givin' me some fucking money... Comprendes?" She took two steps towards me and with a click, a switchblade knife was suddenly pointed straight at my stomach. I looked around, terrified. I wondered where everyone had gone. I wondered how it had gotten so dark so quick.

"Now you gimme your whole fucking wallet, compadre. Now," she said with small stabbing actions towards me. "You betta do it or you never fucking see your fucking train again."

Something took over me. Maybe it was instinct, maybe self-defense, or maybe the culmination of all the shit in my life building up looking for a release, but something snapped. It wasn't fair that my wife had been ripped from my life. It wasn't fair that my friends had disappeared. It wasn't fair that I was a lonesome drunk while the person that murdered them all was out running free. It wasn't fair that now I was the one getting threatened and robbed when all I wanted was some help. I had had enough. My body started trembling and I was aware of two things: the hot tears that ran down my cheeks and the increasing tightness with which I gripped the neck of my bottle.

Fuck it. I swung.

My one-third full bottle of Ketel One slammed against her head with a dull thud. It didn't break. There was no tinkling crash of glass shattering into a million pieces like television had trained me to expect. The woman didn't struggle through the blow and try to retaliate, which had also been the expected behavior from television's life lessons. Instead, she dropped to the sidewalk like the heap of trash that she was. She had fallen onto her side and a small trickle of blood ran out of her ear, making its way across her cheek and down under her nose before dripping into a pool on the ground. Her eyes were closed but fluttered behind the lids like an REM cycle on speed. Her breathing was heavy and snoring sounds escaped from deep within her nasal cavity. At least I knew she was alive. For a moment, I felt the desire to keep hitting her, to punish her for everything bad in my life.

For that one second, everything was her fault. I lifted my foot to stomp on her and I saw a tarnished ring on her left ring finger. She was married to someone. It didn't matter that she was a violent junkie. She had people in her life that depended on her. And I couldn't take that away, not even from her. I stopped mid-step and looked around, saw no one, and ran.

I ran until my legs were rubber and my lungs begged me to stop. Gasping for air, I ducked into an alley to finish the rest of the bottle. I was shaking all over from what I had just done and what I had almost done. The soothing medicine hit my throat and I started to calm down. Out of the corner of my eye, a child's discarded plastic Barbie stuck out of a trash bag, buried in the muck. I finished the entire third of the bottle in one long pull. The effect was immediate and I blacked out.

Between intoxicated flashes of consciousness, I vaguely remembered asking random people for directions. The rest of the time was spent in blackness where I remember nothing, though I somehow stumbled my way back to the train station. I threw up in the handicapped stall in the bathroom and briefly passed out. There were no dreams. I woke up a short time later, rinsed out my mouth, and got on the train.

Chapter 17

Another week passed by and as I had anticipated, Neil was
my lone remaining friend. He sat by himself on the first level
of the train with no one to impress with his boating stories.
I felt bad for him. But it was nothing compared to how bad I
felt for myself, knowing I'd sat across the aisle from my
wife's killer for months, and that it had taken the murder of
four other people before I finally realized it. I was fueled by
only alcohol and revenge. I lost my grip on everything else in
my life that was not Shawn.

"These equations were supposed to be finished last

week. Is everything okay?" Mr. Stark had chosen to take a personal interest in me. I was impressed he made it down here on his own. Julie must have reported the results of her psychobabble bullshit analysis. I would have expected this kind of pseudo concern immediately following Vicky's death, but at that time my performance was at its finest so there was no need for it.

But now work wasn't as important. My new single goal was to find Shawn and make him pay. It was my motivation to board that train every day. And since I had to go somewhere after studying him during the commute, I ended up at work. Nowhere in that plan did it say anything about doing quality work.

I told Mr. Stark that I was just a little distracted. What he didn't know was that by "distracted" I meant not giving a fuck about solving equations. He walked out of the room at about the same time I reached into my desk to grab my flask. The alcohol helped me focus and plan. It allowed me to get creative about what I was going to do about Shawn. I built a new routine. After the flask came the notebook. My suicide attempts and all other meaningless shit was scratched off and replaced with things I wanted to do to Shawn.

1. Swing a sock full of rocks at his face.

2. Slice off his ears and feed them to him.

3. Remove his teeth with a rusty nail and hammer.

4. Rip out his heart with my own hands.

5. Murder his soul.

Then I jotted down a note: "Remember, waste the fucker's life that killed your wife."

I was contemplating the correct spelling of "electrocution" before adding it to the list when Julie popped her head in the door.

"Whatcha doin'?" she asked. It was apparently a day full of caring.

"Not a whole lot. Trying to plan out a few things," I told her, palming the flask and putting it back into the drawer. I hoped that the move was sly enough to not get caught, but it didn't really matter anymore. I reeked like alcohol anyway and I could feel the muscles in my mouth not forming the words the way I intended.

"Oh! That's great! Is there anything I can do? Anything I can help you plan out? I'm pretty good with that stuff."

I didn't really think this was her type of ordeal, but maybe she could be useful.

"Um... I'm actually trying to get in touch with some... uh... old friends, but not sure how to get hold of them... I want to tell them about, you know."

"Oh..." her mouth turned down into a frown. She looked around like the answer was in the air somewhere. She really wanted to help me. The way she was programmed, helping me justified herself. Mission accomplished. "Well, have you tried the Internet? They have a ton of sites dedicated to getting back in touch with people, you know?"

I had no idea what she was talking about but I said yes anyway.

"Hmm.... Also, what about common friends? Is there anyone you know that would know these people?"

"I doubt it." I thought it would sound crazy if I told her my only friends were being murdered one by one, just like my wife had been. Something tugged at me with this thought. In a brief instant I felt two wires almost touch each other but failing to make a connection. It must have been because I had electricity on my mind.

"Oh, that's too bad." Her mouth twisted with a final attempt to think of anything. "You're sure there's no one you know that could get in touch with this group of people?"

Another tug. It was that phrase she used, "group of people," combined with something I had thought about: "my only friends" or "only my friends."

The connection was finally made and a light bulb burned brightly in my head. There were hundreds of random people on the train every day, but Shawn had only gone after those that I had labeled my friends: the specific people I grew to know by watching them. That meant Shawn had watched me watching them before I watched him watching them. What did he want? Was he trying to send me a message since I had figured out that he killed Vicky? That didn't make sense. He could have just come after me. There was another problem to solve. I put it on hold for now as I realized that Shawn was probably still watching me. How he was doing it, I had no idea. He hadn't been on the train lately and I knew nothing about him. It wasn't as if I could just go over to his house, knock on the door, and ask him to come out so I could kick his ass.

"Hello? Hello? You there?" Julie waved a hand in front of my eyes. I shook my head, clearing out the cobwebs. "Thought I lost ya. Your eyes kinda glazed over for a minute. You think of something?" she asked with hopeful excitement on her face.

I had thought of something. I couldn't go over to his house because I didn't know where he lived. But if what I thought was true, then he knew where I lived. He had been there to kill Vicky. If he had been watching me on the train, there was a good chance he was still watching me at home too.

"Yeah, Julie. I did." And just to make her feel better, I added, "I think I just thought of someone. Thanks!"

Her smile beamed from ear to ear. Mission accomplished.

Chapter 18

More alcohol. More hate. More paranoia. Every sound, every squeak, every creak of my house caused my heart to speed up as I expected to confront my wife's killer. It usually turned out to be nothing. But Shawn was out there. I knew he was watching.

The night before, I had been eating another frozen dinner, or maybe it was a sandwich. Suddenly a muffled tapping sound came from the living room behind me. I ignored it for a while and poured another drink. It had been a long day of no significance and I celebrated by getting smashed.

I heard the noise again. It was him. It had to be him this time. The noise was drumming on the window, like someone was bored or impatient. Muffled patterns of four.

One, two, three, four.

One, two, three, four.

The rapid successions of taps had to be fingers. I could almost see it - pinky, ring, middle, and pointer.

One, two, three, four. (Pinky, ring, middle, pointer.)

One, two, three, four. (Pinky, ring, middle, pointer.)

I fought the urge to get up. The last three hundred noises weren't him, why would this time be any different?

One, two, three, four.

One, two, three, four.

One, two, three, four.

It was probably just a branch hitting the glass, caught in a breeze. But the sound got louder, more insistent, more impatient.

Quicker. One, two, three, four, one, two, three, four, one, two, three, four...

Over and over it repeated, begging me to check it out. I

grabbed my bottle and walked to the living room, keeping the lights off so I could see the outside through the window instead of my own reflection. The darkness would also allow me to sneak up on Shawn and catch him in the act. It turned out that being drunk and being sneaky didn't work well together. This was demonstrated when I kicked an empty vodka bottle I had thrown on the floor sometime the day before. Or maybe it had been the previous week. I couldn't remember.

I used every curse word in the book as the bottle spun end over end ahead of me. I leaned over to grab my stubbed toe with my hands, but in my drunken state all I managed to do was hit the wall with my face. Stars spun as I keeled over. The blow had been hard enough to make my head swim and my vision blur even more. The kicked bottle ended its journey with a thud under the window from where I had thought I heard the noise. I sat on the living room couch, holding my stubbed toe in one hand and my swelling face in the other. All the commotion had surely scared Shawn off. I punched the couch, angry about having missed the chance to get my proof. I looked out the window anyway. Sitting on the ledge was a McDonald's bag, its grease stains black under the florescent street lights. The image pulsated in and out of focus, syncing with my throbbing head. I saw that the bag was weighed down, kept it in its place on the ledge. Whatever it was, the weight was heavy enough to refute the gusts of wind blowing the rest of the trash in my lawn around in miniature funnels.

I grabbed my bottle and, taking care not to hurt my swollen toe while I put my slippers on, walked outside to get the bag. I knew I was supposed to look into it; it had been left there for me on purpose. I took a huge gulp from the bottle and slowly uncurled the top of the bag. I looked in and saw one charred green eye looking up at me. I dropped the greasy bag and looked at my hands. I had just enough time to register that the stains were not grease before the world whirled around me like the cyclones of trash and I passed out.

Chapter 19

The next day I awoke on the floor next to my bed, with both the bottle and the bag gone. I wondered for an instant if the previous night had even happened; the whole event had a surreal dreamlike quality to it. The throbbing goose egg on my temple convinced me that it had been real. I was only able to remember what had happened after evoking random photographs of reality, snapshots of certain points in time.

Flash - I saw myself screaming into the air, daring Shawn to show himself.

Flash - I was inside, crawling upstairs on my belly.

Flash - I was in the basement, getting more booze.

Flash - I was outside, ripping the paper bag to shreds.

Flash - I was beating a kitchen chair.

If nothing else, I thought as I made my way out of my memories and into the shower, the bag proved that Shawn was still watching me.

When I boarded the train, Neil was already there and staring out of the window, still alone. Shawn was also there, five rows ahead of him, acting like nothing had happened. My initial instinct to go down there and pummel his face in was trumped by logic. There was no need to rush into something that would most likely get broken up as soon as it started. I would get arrested, Shawn would know I was onto him, and I would never get my chance to make him suffer. If I followed him after the train ride, I would possibly get to impose my revenge on him in a more discreet manner. I reflected on how poorly my last attempt to follow him had gone, but the desire to make him pay without interruptions outweighed it. This was the man that had ruined my life in every way possible, and I wanted him to get everything that he deserved. I moved to a seat on the top row, where he would not be able to see me, but I could still keep an eye on him. I watched Shawn watch Neil for the entire length of the trip. I left a message for Julie to let her know I wasn't going to be in today. This time, when Shawn got off of the train, I was right behind him.

He exited the train and headed in the opposite direction of where I normally went. Seemingly oblivious to anything happening around him he cut through an alley, pausing for a moment to admire some graffiti on the walls. The painted image was a circle of children surrounding two adults, one male and one female, in a courtyard enclosed by buildings. They all were smiling and it appeared that the adults were telling a story or reenacting a play for the children. The alley opened up to a street, and Shawn walked two more blocks north and three blocks west. Then a quick right and then two more blocks north. I kept a very accurate mental note of his exact path so I wouldn't get lost in unfamiliar territory again; my last adventure to an unknown place replayed in my mind like a TV show. I shuddered when I thought about the dull thud that had knocked out that woman. I couldn't believe I had been so out of my mind, so drunk that I had actually hurt someone.

Shawn finally stopped at a strip of offices all in a row. The particular office he stood in front of was plain, consisting of only a single glass door and walls that were floor to ceiling glass panels. The glass door had some words spelled out in white letters but I was too far away to see what they said. The giant glass windows had heavy, white curtains preventing those outside from seeing in. I was very cautious. This office could be the place he had taken Rob, Gina, Frank, and Sheila to do whatever he had done to them in real life. Knowing what this monster was capable of in my dreams, I imagined it was a shop full of prison rehabs selling chainsaws and guns. I waited until the door completely shut behind him before I went up for a closer look. The letters spelled out "Dr. Griffin, Dentist." Either Shawn was a dentist or he had been taking the train to one every day for the last three months. And his teeth didn't look that bad. I rolled this new information around in my head, impressed by the genius of it. It was the perfect cover-up. No one would ever suspect a prestigious man such as a dentist to be a murderer. With all of the drilling and teeth pulling, he obviously wouldn't have an aversion to the blood he spilled while killing.

I opened the door, careful to palm the little golden bell tied to the handle to prevent it from ringing as I entered. I looked around. Shawn had already gone to the exam rooms in back. I was in a waiting room with two other patients. A dark-skinned receptionist sat at a desk behind a sliding glass window. No one looked up at me when I entered the office. Like the front of the building, the room itself was plain. On the walls, there were only the generic pictures of fields, old trees, and dirty flowers that seem to hang in every dentist's office. The faded browns, yellows, and pinks suggested that they had been hanging there for quite some time. The television in the corner silently predicted the parental status of promiscuous men, but no one was watching. Personally, I had already seen this episode. Magazines were scattered on tables that separated uncomfortable chairs from more uncomfortable chairs. All the pieces of a waiting room. It was all too predictable. I took a seat.

"Can I help you?" a muffled voice called out to someone from behind the sliding glass window. "Excuse me, sir, do you have an appointment?" The voice was talking to me. Quite uncomfortably, I told her I did not.

"Well, you need to fill out these forms before you can see the dentist." She said this without looking at me, like she'd done it a million times before.

I took the forms clasped to a clipboard with a pen and walked to an uncomfortable chair. I wasn't sure I wanted to fill out these forms. I wasn't sure I was ready to confront Shawn yet. I wasn't sure what I was even doing here. But I had to act cool, so I started writing anything down, just to look like I was writing something.

Name: Sock full of rocks

Address: Slice off ears

Reason for visit: Pull out teeth

As I regurgitated my latest notebook entries onto the

form, I thought about what I was really here for –
information on this sick fucker.

"Excuse me, ma'am," I asked, suddenly very friendly.

"Mmm-hmm?" she asked, still not looking at me,
writing something more important that required far more
attention.

"I was wondering if you can tell me if... Sh... um...
Dr... uh... Griffin has any other offices aside from this
location?"

"Nope."

"Uh... okay. Do you, um, have a card with his
information? I'm actually just researching dentists right now
so I don't really need to see him yet." I thought my answer
was pretty convincing until I saw her stop writing.

She made a point of putting down her pen very
gently and folded her hands. Her head still pointed down to
whatever she had been writing and only her eyes looked up
at me with a blink. Mouth closed, she inhaled through her
nose as she ran her tongue over the front of her teeth. Her
upper lip rippled from right to left and it looked like a

caterpillar was crawling over them. Her eyes shifted to the right with a slight nod of her head. I saw that there was an oversized white wooden tooth holding an entire stack of business cards on the counter. Written across the tooth was the word "Information."

"Oh, right." I said and took a card. "Thanks."

Her eyes widened, her forehead crinkled, and she tilted her head back as if to say, "Yep. Sure." Then she went back to her business, picking up her pen as carefully as she had set it down.

The card didn't have all of the information I needed. "Does... Dr. Griffin have a home or emergency number? I don't live around here and I would need a way to get hold of him during non-business hours... in case of a... tooth emergency. I live a couple hours north of here in... well, you probably never heard of it, but it's by that giant new marina they're building."

The pen barely made a sound as she set it down again. This time her entire head pointed at me as she interlocked her fingers and balanced her elbows on the table. I had her full attention now. "You don't say. What is it with you people all the way up there wanting to travel all the way into the city?" The monotonous tone was void of any excitement.

"What do you mean by 'you people'?" I asked.

"Well. Not that it's any of your business, but Dr. Griffin moved up that way about six months ago."

"Is that so?" Now I was getting somewhere.

"He's also by that marina, and he's always complaining that whatever they're doing causes his water to stop working, despite living right by some giant water tower. Serves him right though, living that far away. That's what I say. Anyway, any more questions?" She picked up her pen and I knew there would not be any more questions, despite her not answering my original one. But I did know the water tower she was talking about, and I now knew part of Shawn's real name. It was time to get to know Dr. Griffin.

Chapter 20

I hustled back to the train station, stopping for a bottle of Stoli along the way. On the train home, I celebrated my newly found information by drinking it. Despite my decent buzz, the ride still took forever, and each passing minute felt like an hour. My mind raced as a plan clicked into place with minimal effort. I would go to the village hall to find out his address. Then I would stake him out like they do on television. Then the man that had killed my wife and my friends would pay with his life.

The train finally pulled into the station after what

felt like six days, but was really only two hours. The water tower the receptionist had mentioned was only one town away from the station, so my next stop would be the village hall. The task of getting his address was not nearly as difficult as I had thought. I had an elaborate scheme all planned, where I would say I had the same name but lived in a different town. I was going to say that I had been getting his mail and wanted to bring it to him before the bills became past due. But when I gave the lady behind the desk the name Dr. Griffin, she looked up the information in her computer before I had a chance to get into my story. She wrote his street address on the back of an envelope and slid it across the desk to me. That was a benefit of living within a group of small towns – no one ever expected any foul play.

I drove to his house. I had a few hours before he would be home from work and I wanted to find out more about him. I turned into the driveway of a ranch-style house in what seemed to be the older part of town. Tall trees covered the entire house in shade. The lack of sun explained why the lawn was spotted with crabgrass growing in hard packed dirt. The dark brown stained siding of the house was riddled with gaping holes where hunks of wood had been ripped out from years of wear. Overgrown bushes prevented a clear passage to the front door, but I somehow managed. The front porch was covered in dirt and dead leaves. I had expected more from a rich dentist.

I peered through the fogged glass in the front door. For such a humble exterior, the inside of the house did actually seem like a rich dentist lived there. Hardwood floors lead the way to an immaculate furniture set that was far from anything bought at IKEA. Shawn's furniture looked as though a forest had been chopped down and carved into pieces by Mongolian monks. Just past the living room, I could see a gigantic television surrounded by a multitude of black boxes. I assumed they were a DVD player, surround sound, a cable box, some sort of video game system, and who knows what else. This fucker had everything, and because of him, I had nothing. I fought the urge to break in and destroy everything he had, just as he had destroyed everything I had. But that wouldn't have been close to good enough for me. I needed more. So I simply took advantage of the privacy shrubbery and pissed on his doorknob.

Chapter 21

The weekend was spent drinking, planning, and drinking more. A morbid excitement came over me that I had not expected. I was actually looking forward to this. Ideas spun through my head as fast as the alcohol spun through my veins. I thought about staging a robbery at his place. Breaking in and ending it right then and there. Another tragic victim of today's godless society. However, the more I thought about it, the plan left too many unanswered questions and would result in an investigation that could possibly end on my doorstep. Also, it was far too lenient a plan for what he did to me. I wanted him to suffer at my hands. And I wanted him to know it was me. I finally decided on doing it here, at my house. It was the place he had killed Vicky and I knew he had been back at least one time to put that bag on my window ledge. My paranoia was justified. Each and every bump in the night was him, watching me, fucking with me, seeing the result of his dirty deeds. I would wait for him to show up again and then I would have him. That was step one. I would deal with step two when the time came. I went to work on Monday with some sense of relief, or at least some sense of direction.

"Hey, how are things going?" Julie asked. Her good intended interest in me had gone well past annoying.

"Okay, I suppose," I said, trying to give her the most I'm-really-really-busy look I could give. It wasn't hard since my work had been piling up for weeks and I was really-really-busy.

"I just wanted to see if you found those friends you were looking for. You know, from your past."

It took me a moment to remember. "Oh yeah, not

yet, but I definitely made some promising phone calls and am waiting for them to call back." Hoping she just wanted a fix of praise before leaving, I added, "Thanks so much for your help. I owe it all to you."

"Oh, not a problem at all. I'm glad I was able to help."

She lingered. There was more coming.

"Hey, I had another question. Do you want to come over after work for dinner sometime? We've both been pretty worried about you spending so much time alone."

I totally blanked on her fiancé's name despite her telling me five million times before. "I appreciate your... both of your concern. But I'm not sure if I'll be able to make it," I replied, hoping that would be the end of it.

"But I didn't even ask about a day or time... How could you tell me no if you don't even know the date and time?" She was really trying my patience.

"I'm just very busy this whole week with all of the work I've been missing," I said, still trying to be as nice as I could. What didn't she get? I felt panic and anxiety start to set in again. The walls were closing in and it was like she had become a fifty-foot giant in the room, smothering me, not letting me breathe, not letting me move. What did she want from me? I needed her away from me.

"If during the week's no good, how about on the weekend? We really wouldn't mind hav-"

"Fine," I interrupted, not caring what she suggested, just trying to get her the hell away from me, to give myself some space so I could breathe again. "How about this Friday?" I blurted out without really thinking about what it meant. I think I meant to say, "Shut the fuck up bitch, you are so goddamn annoying with your pretend concern, built up to make yourself feel better about helping someone," but it came out wrong. I just wanted to shut her up.

"That would be great! Pete and I would be so delighted," she exclaimed without giving me a second to think about what I had actually said.

I paused. "Who's Pete?" I asked. What the fuck was I doing? My mind stalled. For a second I thought that might be Shawn's real name. I should have looked that up.

"He's... my fiancé. You knew that." Her eyebrows pulled together.

"Right. Sorry, Pete, right. I thought you said something else." What just happened? What the hell was wrong with me?

"Okay, so what time do you want to come over?"

Fuck. I wouldn't be able to watch out for Shawn if I was in the city at Julie's. "I have a better idea," I started, as I saw the only way to salvage anything from this situation. "How about you and... um... Pete come over to my place for dinner? You've been so... uh... helpful through this trying time that it would be the least I could do to repay you." This would at least allow me to keep an eye on the house in case Shawn showed up.

"I think that would be alright as long as it's not a problem for you."

"Not at all. Around seven o'clock?" I smiled as best I could, but I actually felt like pushing her out through the doorway. And by doorway, I meant window.

"That would be fine. Need us to bring anything?"

"Nope. I'll have it all taken care of." There was an awkward pause as we were both out of things to say, staring at each other. "Well..." I nodded at the ever-increasing pile of papers on my desk.

"Oh, sure, sure. See you Friday!" She turned around and walked out of my office.

I leaned back in my chair and looked up into the fluorescent sea of no answers. I kept telling myself that I would at least be around in case Shawn made an appearance.

I got home that night and started cleaning. Because of my poorly thought out suggestion during my little panic attack, I now had four days to get my place looking decent. At the present, it was literally a garbage dump. Empty bottles of vodka, cups, plates, clothes, and garbage lined the floors, wall to wall. At some point during my nights of binging, I'd resorted to throwing the empties anywhere. I didn't care as long as I could sleep without dreaming; as long as I could sleep, period.

I found bottles behind the couch, under the kitchen table, and even a Grey Goose liter in the oven. I vaguely remembered that night. I had put it in the oven to hide it from Shawn, whom I was convinced was in my house that night. I had heard noises coming from upstairs; his voice whispering, threatening me. After I had hidden the bottle, I tore my place apart armed with a baseball bat, hitting anything I thought moved. I finally climbed out onto the little terrace attached to the guest bedroom and sat there in silence, figuring he would never find me out there. I had woken up freezing on that terrace.

After most of the bottles and trash had been picked up, I decided that was enough for one night. I still had three more days. I decided to eat dinner and then wait for Shawn. I had a feeling that he might show up tonight. I left the television off so that I would be able to hear him sneaking around, certain that he would show up at any minute. I sat under the kitchen's solitary light bulb, illuminating only the table and the plate I had set on it. The rest of the house was dark. I sat. I ate. I drank. I listened. When I was done eating, I cleaned up and sat some more. And drank some more. There was no sound anywhere, inside or outside.

Then I heard it. A single floorboard creaked under what could only be the weight of someone taking a step. Snapping out of a memory of our honeymoon in Mexico, my heart raced and my palms went sweaty. The noise came from upstairs. I grabbed the largest knife I could from the knife block on the counter and tiptoed to the foyer stairs as silent as a cat. How did he get in the house and upstairs without making any noise? He must have gotten in while I was thinking about Vicky. I stood at the bottom landing for an eternity, listening for another step. I heard nothing. No creaks, no squeaks, no Shawn. In the stillness of the foyer, I was certain it was him and that he had somehow sneaked back out. I went upstairs to find some sort of evidence that he had been there. Each step sent pulses of adrenaline through my veins. There was nothing. I spent the rest of the night on the stairs, knife in hand, listening. That's where I woke up the next morning.

Chapter 22

Neil had regressed from looking merely lonely to utterly abandoned. He sat in his usual seat with his arms crossed in front of his chest, looking out the window. I wanted to tell him that soon the loss of his friends would be avenged. But I couldn't tell him what I was planning to do. I couldn't tell anyone. The rest of the train ride was uneventful. I was half looking around for Shawn, almost expecting him to show his face. He didn't.

Work had slipped into an uninterrupted rhythm. It seems that my invitation to have Julie and whatshisname over for dinner had earned me the rest of the week without her pestering. I was almost able to get caught up on all of my work. Equation after equation resolved itself on the papers in front me. X equals 15 apples in a barrel, X equals 147 turns of a clock's key before breaking it, X equals 3 minutes the average chicken can stay in flight. Before I knew it, it was already fifteen minutes past the time I needed to leave in order to catch my regular train back home. I sat back in my chair and rubbed my eyes. Resting for just a few minutes more, I eventually summoned up the energy to stand up, grab my coat, and leave. I couldn't afford to take a later train with all the cleaning I had to do.

When I boarded the train for the ride home, there was only one seat left on the upper level and it was in the half of the row that faced towards the center aisle. I was going to be stuck across from another person, having to acknowledge their existence. And as it turned out, it was a person I already knew. Shawn. I couldn't believe it. He was sitting directly across from me and obviously ignoring me. His black Converse shoes rested against the guard rail that prevented passengers from falling onto the seats below. His long black trench coat was wrapped tightly around him and his black hat was pulled down over his eyes. He didn't want to face me. But at this point I knew better. He knew what car I sat in. He knew I sat in the top row. He was fucking with me. He had been in my house last night and was now sitting across from me in order to rub it in.

It took everything I had to refrain from jumping to the other side of the train and ending it there. I needed to be more discreet than that. I spent the entire ride with my anger and hatred building. My next step mapped itself out in my mind. I originally wanted to hurt him, but this son of a bitch deserved worse. My life had become so numb from all of the pain, suffering, and alcohol that the word "murder" didn't even have a sense of finality to it anymore. Killing Shawn would be just another something to do, another life lesson shown on my very own television show. The only satisfaction would be in knowing that he couldn't hurt anyone else the way he hurt me.

I had a brief inclination that I was crossing a line somewhere. Did I really have what was needed to take a life? To do something that could never be taken back? I thought of my Vicky nailed to the floor, soaking in her own blood.

Yes, I did. I had what it took to do it.

I would dedicate the rest of my pathetic life to killing Shawn. And it would be soon.

I decided to follow him home. I'd had enough of waiting for him to come to me; it was bullshit. I was going to end this, end him.

When he stepped off the train, I made sure to mark which car he walked to. It was nothing spectacular; an old, beat up silver Oldsmobile. The body of the car was rusting around the wheels. As the door was opened to capacity, it creaked until there was a plastic-on-metal snap. Not the type of car I expected a dentist to drive but easy enough to follow. Although I already knew where he lived, I followed his car in case he didn't go straight home. And he didn't. He made a stop at the grocery store. I followed him inside, making sure I was at least fifty or so steps behind him, ready to jump into the closest aisle should he turn around. Someone crafty enough to get away with five murders might realize that he was being followed.

He didn't appear to buy anything of any significance;

some pasta noodles and a bottle of wine. Following him into the liquor department, I was a kid in a candy store. I picked up a bottle of Stoli to kill time in the car while I watched Shawn's house that night. He didn't appear to see me, even when I used the self-checkout kiosk right next to him. I followed him to the parking lot and then back to his house.

Shawn's life seemed as lonely as mine, minus the microwave dinners. I sat with my vodka outside, watching him through his kitchen window. Instead of turning on the television, he flipped on his giant expensive stereo system and played a CD. It was Beethoven or Mozart, I couldn't tell for sure. I saw a gentleman with white hair playing piano on the CD case that he tossed onto the couch like a Frisbee. Soon Shawn would be dead, just like that composer.

Each step he took in his house radiated hate through my veins. There he was, alive and well, content with his life after killing my wife and those people from the train. The only thing keeping me somewhat calm was the constant intake of alcohol. Each time I got the feeling that I wanted to rush in and tackle him, I took a drink.

I started wondering why he did it, how he did it, and

what he did with the bodies. Vicky's was obvious. He left her pinned to my kitchen floor. But what about the others? Though sometimes blurred, there was still a line between my dreams and reality. I knew what he'd done in my dreams but what did he do in real life? Where were the bodies? If he had left them all pinned to their respective floors, it would have been all over the news. And I'd heard nothing.

I snapped back to the present and didn't see Shawn any more. He couldn't have gone far, judging by the noodles boiling in a pot and an empty skillet heating up on the burner next to it. I spun around quickly, suddenly convinced that he was sneaking up on me. But there was no one behind me.

Then I saw him. He walked back into view, through a door just past the kitchen. At first glance, I thought the door had opened to a pantry but now I saw that it actually lead to a basement.

He carried a pile of red meat on a plate. The meat was covered with plastic wrap and it looked frosted over, as if he had just pulled it out of a freezer. The entire ensemble looked homemade. I had heard of people buying meat in bulk to save money and then separating it into smaller servings at home.

Trying to hold the plate steady while he removed his shoes, he used the toe of his right shoe to push down the heel of his left one. He almost lost his balance. As he steadied himself, a stringy vein slipped out from beneath the plastic wrap and dripped a single drop of blood onto his bare white sock. The last time I'd seen blood on a sock was when I had found Vicky's body. I focused solely on the single red blemish soaking into his sock, lost in a memory.

He took off the other shoe and crossed the floor to the stove. He unwrapped the plastic and scraped the meat into the hot skillet. The sizzling and popping of the fat turned my stomach as I thought of Sheila in the cave. Was that the answer to what he did with the bodies? Controlling my gag reflex, I theorized what had really happened to the people from the train; how he was getting rid of the evidence. Was that even possible? I thought about the blood dripping from the vein. Meat bought in bulk doesn't have any veins. For the sake of my train friends' families, I hoped I was wrong. Bon appetit. The ground rushed up at me and I fainted.

When I came to, I figured I had only been out about ten to twenty minutes since Shawn was sitting at his kitchen table eating. With each bite he took, that dry, gagging feeling resonated against the back of my throat. Images of what he did to Vicky flashed through my mind. Her mutilated neck and her hands nailed to the floor. I watched him as he washed down a mouthful with a sip of wine and a smile. I was filled with a rage that all the Stoli in the world wouldn't fix.

I looked around for the bottle I had dropped when I fainted. I found it, picked it up, and holding it at arm's length, looked through it. In double vision, once from the vodka in my system and twice from the alcohol still in the bottle, I saw the rough outline of a rectangle near the ground. I dropped the bottle to my side, shook away the buzzing in my head, and looked again. My vision somewhat cleared and I saw the rectangle was actually a window into Shawn's basement. Two dark panes of glass stared at me, like eyes of a face buried in the ground. The window itself was framed in wood, aged by the many years it spent watching the neighborhood, learning and keeping its secrets while it rotted away. Looking closer on my hands and knees, I saw it was locked by only a small metal hook screwed into the frame. Without a sound, I pushed on the darkened glass and the screw easily slid out while the window opened in.

I lowered myself feet-first into the basement, sliding backwards on my stomach. My toes wavered in the air, searching for a floor some distance below me. Holding on to the rickety frame with my hands, my feet finally touched down. I looked out the window once more to ensure no one had seen my little maneuver. Almost as an afterthought, I grabbed the vodka bottle from the ground and dragged it in behind me.

I turned and faced a dark, cool room. The rock walls reminded me of the cave I had last seen Sheila in, damp and reeking of death. The floor was cement, broken up by cracks spider webbing from one wall to another. As quiet as I could be, I walked over to a large stainless steel freezer that sat by two by fours framing the stairs leading up to the rest of the house. The floor around the freezer was stacked with too many shoes for one person to have. I thought of the single drop of blood stained onto Shawn's sock and my stomach lurched. I didn't want to look in the freezer. I knew what was in there.

Directly across from the freezer against a cement wall, was an old dentist chair stained with what looked like dark oil but I knew wasn't. It sat under a single can light clamped to a pipe in the unfinished ceiling. An orange extension cord hung down and ran out of the room. I'd never heard of a dentist practicing his craft in the comfort of his own dirty basement. A shelf lining the wall above the chair was filled with bottles of chloroform and jars of teeth. There must have been ten jars total. I assumed at least four jars were new.

The pipe holding the can light shook as water flowed through it from the kitchen sink above. He was cleaning up after dinner and if his life truly resembled mine, he would soon be going to bed. I decided the best thing to do was to wait until he went to sleep for the night. I waited for ten minutes by counting to six hundred as calmly and controlled as I could after the crack of light disappeared from beneath the door at the top of the stairs. It would have been plenty of time for him to get into bed and fall asleep.

I walked up the stairs, holding the bottle of vodka by the neck, to use as a hammer in case I miscalculated what the lights going out meant. The basement door had not been shut all the way, so I only had to push it open and hope it didn't squeak. It didn't. I stepped into the kitchen and smelled the lingering aroma of something like greasy fried chicken mixed with a twinge of sweet barbeque. It hung in the air like a tangible fog. I took a drink from my bottle just to get the taste of it out of my mouth. I felt my way around the kitchen using my memory of what I had seen from the outside. The dim yellow glow from the street lights didn't help at all.

With my back against the wall for support, my fingertips slid across the wall and arrived at a set of stairs leading to the second floor. I figured it would be best to crawl, rather than walk, up the stairs to decrease the chances of falling down them in my inebriated state, so I got on all fours and began my ascent. As I crawled like a dog, it dawned on me that I was lucky Shawn didn't have any pets that would have alerted him to my presence. I continued until I got to the second floor landing. Out of the three doorways there, only one of them was closed, presumably because it was his room. I panicked for a moment when I imagined that he locked his door. But I didn't lock my doors when I was home alone so it was reasonable to assume he didn't either. When I turned the knob, the door opened. I silently sighed in relief.

The door swung open with a long slow creak that left me frozen where I stood. There was no disruption in his breathing pattern. The mound of blankets over him rose and fell in a constant rhythm with the breaths he took. I walked in slow motion over to the side of the bed and stood over him. I looked down into his face. There he was. The man that changed my life forever. The man that killed my wife and four other innocent people. The man that took everything from me and left me with nothing. He was the reason I had become a lonely, suicidal, drunk, depressed, worthless piece of shit. And now I wanted to murder him.

My grip on the bottle tightened. As I swung it down, I thought of the woman who had tried to rob me in the alley. I expected that he would take the hit and remain unconscious. I was wrong. Different people have different reactions to getting hit in the head with heavy glass objects. Plus, my blunt weapon did not strike where I wanted it to. I aimed for the left temple, but what I hit was the top of his left ear.

"OW! What the heck?" he yelled. He jolted straight up in his bed, cradling his ear with both hands. "What, what, who... Oh my god, who are you and wha... wha... wha..."

Instinct took over. Without even thinking, I backhanded the bottle across the unprotected side of his face. This time, the hit felt solid and heavy, like a bowling ball had been dropped from a roof onto hard packed dirt. And the aim was dead on. His glazed eyes looked past me into some other world and rolled up into their sockets. His unconscious body withered snakelike back into his bed and he began to snore loudly. To make sure he was really out, I started slapping his face with my hands as hard as I could. It felt good.

"You mother fucker," I spat at him. "I'm going to end your fucking life, you piece of fucking shit." Slap, slap,

slap.

I lost track of time. Seeing the dark red blood stream out from his ears onto the sheets, I forced myself to stop.

The room spun and I gasped for air to catch my breath. I stared at his limp body, and between long drinks I tried to recollect the past few minutes. The details already seemed hazy and fading with each passing second. Concentrating on a table lamp to stop the room from spinning, I stood over this unconscious, bleeding person as I held the weapon in my hand. I had to get out of there. I wanted to abandon the plan and run, but he had seen me. Even if it was dark and he had just woken up, I couldn't take any chances. I had come too far to turn back now.

I thought about keeping him tied up here but didn't know if someone would come to check in on him. Maids, family, lovers. I figured by the time anyone called him it would all be over, one way or another. However, if I kept him here I would have to constantly travel back and forth. I finally decided my house was the best place to bring him. It was not lost on me that my house was also the very place this had all started.

I wrapped him up in his own bedding, then half rolled and half threw him down the stairs. A brainless "Ugh" escaped his body as it hit the floor. I stood there, the bottle tensed in my hand in case the fall had awakened him, but he remained still. The sound had just been the air forced out of his lungs from the impact. The trepidation of him stirring reminded me to grab some chloroform from the shelf in the basement next to the teeth. I couldn't very well have this asshole waking up in my house and screaming bloody murder.

I pushed, pulled, and kicked him out the door and into the trunk of my car. I was fairly confident that no one had seen me. It was the middle of the night with only the basement windows keeping watch. And they weren't going to tell.

Chapter 23

I woke up the next morning in my own bed, exhausted and initially unsure of what actually happened the previous night. I might have had another dream. My head pounded and it felt like a hard chunk of sand had replaced my tongue. I was late for work and rushed through my morning routine so I could get to the train on time. Through the grogginess of a massive hangover, I again remembered things in flashes as I got ready. Brushed my teeth. Followed Shawn. Took a piss. Watched him eat. Showered. Sneaked in the basement window. As I tied my shoes, the rest came back to me. I had a house guest in my basement. I ran downstairs to double check. Shawn was still there and still knocked out. His appearance there was surreal, like I was watching a movie. In that movie, I had held a washcloth soaked in chloroform over his face for a few minutes. From what I had researched, that would keep him sedated anywhere from six to eight hours or possibly forever. I left for work, not really believing that actually happened.

I saw Neil and no longer felt sorry for him. I felt happiness. Or maybe it was redemption. Either way, I knew that I had saved at least one person from the maniac in my basement. Neil had survived; he was safe. I arrived at work in a better mood than I had been in for months. I sat down to hammer through some equations when Julie came in and tried to ruin my day.

"We're so excited about coming over Friday night. Are you sure you don't want us to bring anything?"

Fuck. Fuck. FUCK. I had forgotten that I had invited Julie and whatshisname over for dinner on Friday. I had been alone for so long and all of a sudden I was Mr. Fucking Popular. I quickly tried to think of a believable excuse to get out of it.

She must have seen me thinking. "Don't even try to bail on this. You need this. We're coming." Busted.

"No, not at all. We're still on. Seven o'clock sharp." It actually might have been a blessing in disguise. All I had to do was keep Shawn quiet in the basement during dinner and I would have my alibi in case the cops ever started sniffing around trying to associate me with Shawn's disappearance. Not that it would ever happen, but it would be best to have one just in case.

"You know it." Her smile was so wide it almost split her face in two.

"OK. I'll see you then." I wanted to split her face in two.

As the day wore on, I thought about what I had done. Being at work, removed from the situation, put the whole ordeal into perspective. I had a moment of clarity, an insight into reality. Suddenly, I dreaded going home. I had kidnapped someone and planned to kill him. What if I got caught? What if someone saw me take his body from his house? What if the cops were waiting for me when I got home? I reached for the bottle I had hidden in my desk drawer and took a long swallow, trying to answer all of these questions. Perhaps the answers were at the bottom of the bottle this time. By the time I was able to see they weren't, my morals had disappeared. My mind flashed the picture from Yosemite where Vicky and I had tried to find the restroom. One of the best pictures we've ever taken together. Fury swept in and consumed my body like someone had shot a bullet of hate directly into my heart. Fuck Shawn. I could do this. I would do this.

In addition to that bottle of booze filling me with liquid courage, it also gave me enough focus to get some work done. I alternated between solving equations and referencing my notebook that I had created precisely for this situation. I took sips of alcohol each time I flipped between the two.

Swing a sock full of rocks at his face. Drink.

Solve for X. Drink.

Slice off ears and feed them to him. Drink.

Find derivative of Y. Drink.

Remove his teeth with a rusty nail and hammer.

Drink.

I multitasked myself into a good buzz by five o'clock and then it was time to go home. I was ready. I had hardened myself to do what was needed. I was a rock. I would have no mercy for this mother fucker. Tired from the night before, I ended up nodding off on the train.

And that's when I lost Neil.

Chapter 24

This dream picked up where Frank's death had left off. I was
back at the pier next to the wooden shack I had hidden
behind before getting on Neil's death boat. I turned around
just in time to see the boat sinking into the black water,
surrounded by rotting shark corpses. Frank's impaled head
was pointed straight up towards the gray sky. The suction of
the boat sliding backwards into the depths of the water was
also taking a few lifeless husks with it, forever to be buried
with Frank. I walked into the shack and saw Neil next to the
trap door, huddled under some of the paint-stained tarps

to cover gaping holes. The ground was hard packed dirt, with a giant stack of hay blocks in the corner.

Above the haystack, a single can light was turned to face the center of the barn, creating a giant ellipse on the floor. The orange extension cord to the light ran out of a window and I wondered if it was the same light from Shawn's basement. The rest of the barn was a wide open empty room; no tools, no tables, nothing. The only door to the barn was padlocked with a heavy chain, so this had to be where Neil had ended up. That meant Shawn was also here. But I couldn't see either of them.

I crawled out of the vent, stood up, and brushed myself off. I placed both of my hands on the small of my lower back to hold it in place while I leaned back and popped the joints that had tightened from my crawling. As my back made a sound like bubble wrap twisted in an eager child's hand, I glanced up at the wall I just crawled out of. Since I couldn't see the face of this wall from within the vent, I hadn't noticed how completely different it was from the others. This wall was finished and painted bright yellow, and the color made it look even more out of place than it did just by being finished.

High up in the corner, where the yellow wall met the planked roof, what looked like a bundle of mummies wrapped in dirty gray bandages hung from chains. But unlike mummies, their appendages were fully extended; they were giant Xs with heads. The heads themselves were not wrapped. Dried out decaying skulls with empty eye sockets and rotting teeth smiled the smile of the dead. The gray wrapping stood out against the yellow wall like a sore thumb. Taking a broader look, the entire perimeter of the ceiling was lined with these mummified five-pointed figures.

I also saw that in the middle of the ceiling, hanging right above the ellipse of light in the center of the room, was Neil. He was wrapped up to his nose in the same gray bandage-like material the others were, except he was alive and conscious. His eyes darted all over the room, fearfully looking for a way out. I was in plain sight but his eyes passed over me; he couldn't see me. I shouted up at him but he couldn't hear me. Instead, he was lowered down into the egg-shaped sphere of light until his feet barely brushed the ground. A buzzing sound, like garbage flies and kazoos, consumed the room. Neil did hear this sound. The gray bandages over his crotch darkened and liquid dripped through them onto the floor, first beading up then soaking into the thirsty dirt.

The buzzing increased in volume until it was no longer a sound but a wave of vibration that shook the walls. My eyes shook in their sockets, blurring my vision. The bodies on the ceiling began swinging to and fro from the vibration, hitting the walls, thumping to the beat of some unheard song. The uncontrolled way they danced made it seem like the source of the buzz was within them; it was a rattle of the dead. Neil twisted and struggled to get free, but all he managed to do was swing like a pendulum back and forth over his own puddle of piss.

A body in the upper left corner of the yellow wall was buzzing louder than the rest, slamming itself against the wall so hard that it almost hit the rafters on the rebound. It lay still for a moment, shook, and then exploded. More specifically, its stomach exploded. With the sharp, dry pop of a brown paper bag slammed between two fists, the bandages ripped open and a shower of what looked like small pebbles blasted outward towards the center of the room where Neil hung. A majority of them hit me in the face and chest as they descended. So much for being completely invisible.

Something tickled the back of my neck and I slapped it. I felt thick goo and pulled my hand away from my wet neck. My entire palm was filled with chunky red jelly surrounded by still twitching hairy sticks. I looked down and saw the pebbles that scuttled towards the ellipse of light were not pebbles at all. The mummy-like corpse hanging in the rafters had expunged hundreds of deformed spiders into the room. And they were all crawling to Neil.

I looked up at the creature and the eye sockets of the mummy's skull glowed red as the corpse came to life. The violent escape of the spiders left its cracked ribs facing outward; they looked like giant skeletal fingers stabbed through the back, jutting out through the front. The ribs started to wiggle and writhe like a centipede flipped on its back, trying to right itself. Drumming helplessly in the air, the gray wrapping loosened and fell off, revealing the corpse's true form.

Kicking away the spiders that tried to bite me, I was

helpless to turn away from the creature I saw. As the last of the gray wrapping swirled through the air to the ground in slow motion, I saw that the end of the outstretched arms had crab-like pincers instead of hands. They were opening and closing in the air, pinching for the first time in ages. The appendages I had thought were feet were actually two separate tails with a sharp deadly point at each end, like a scorpion's. The red eyes glowed brighter and a long black tongue lapped in and out between the rotting teeth like a snake trying to breathe. Using its claws, it spun around on the chain and its wriggling ribs took hold of the wall. I realized that the exploded ribs were actually spider-like legs. It easily cut through the chain with its claw and started walking down the wall.

As the aberration stepped its way down the wall, the other husks stopped bouncing and exploded. The domino effect of corpses exploding and thrusting out living crawling spiders created an opaque cloud of blackness. With each rapid bang, thousands of spiders were flung through the air, raining down everywhere. Once the air cleared, the entire barn floor was covered in a black sea of moving creatures, all making their way to Neil as he hung in the center of the room.

I waded through the ankle-high mass of spiders towards the haystack. Every time I lifted a leg, spiders were flung in all directions like corn kernels in hot oil. Every time I stepped down, it produced a crunch, pop, or slide before my next step. By the time I made it to the haystack, all of the corpses had exploded and the living red-eyed creatures were slowly crawling down the wall after their excreted spawn.

The first spiders to make it into the circle of light crawled up Neil's hanging body. His eyes filled with dread and he was swinging back and forth as hard as he could, attempting to escape or at least throw them off. Since the buzzing had ceased, all I heard were high pitched muffled screams coming from his covered mouth. No words, just sounds. The spiders continued to crawl up Neil; each new wave forcing the previous ones higher up his body. There were so many of them that his feet and legs were completely coated in black. The mass made its way up to his waist, chest, and then his neck. Eventually, his entire body was covered in black crawling spiders; only his darting eyes were visible. Then the spiders tore through the wrapping over his mouth and began to climb in.

As the spiders filed in, filling Neil's mouth, I could hear the click-clacking of a hundred typewriters as the corpses' ribs stepped off the wall and onto the floor. The giant scorpion-like creatures made their way to the center of the barn, herding their offspring towards Neil like cattle into a pen. Neil's eyes glazed over in shock and his face reddened as he choked from loss of air. From the weight of the spiders invading his body, his midsection pushed outward and swelled. I tried not to think about how many spiders must have entered him to engorge like that.

The corpse creatures encircled Neil. He barely breathed; his lungs had no room to expand or contract. With a quick scissoring motion, one of the monsters reached a claw into the circle and sliced off Neil's left arm just below the elbow. The arm landed in the urine-soaked dirt below him with a dull thud, no longer a living entity but instead a hunk of dead meat. Neil's head thrust back in pain, but he was unable to produce any sound. The only thing coming out of his mouth was a sea of little hairy legs waving at their parents. The veins of his neck were tight cords pulled taught in pain. The blood vessels in his eyeballs broke and tears of blood streamed down his face and into his mouth, coating the spiders and sending them into more of a frenzy. The beast that had sliced off his arm curled its left tail over its head in a wide arc and stuck the fallen arm with its pointed end. It raised the arm over its head, as if wanting to answer a question. Then it let whatever blood was left in the arm drain onto its red-eyed skull before inserting the entire thing into its mouth and swallowing it. I saw Neil's college football ring sparkle once before it passed through the rotted teeth.

As if this were some sort of permissive gesture in the language of the damned, the other creatures sliced off and ate Neil's other arm and both legs. When they were done feasting, all that was left of Neil was a hanging placental sac filled with their young. Blood squirted and dripped onto the floor, mixing with the urine. The ground became a soft, muddy soup of Neil's liquids, spreading out until it filled the entire wide ellipse of light surrounding him.

The newly softened ground shook as it split apart

and chunks of mud crumbled to the sides of the spinning figure rising out of it. The spinning motion slowed to a stop as Shawn fully emerged from the earth. He wore his long black trench coat and hat. Somewhere on his journey through the tunnel, he obtained the wooden staff and was now using it to shoo away the scorpion beasts. He paused for a moment, twisted the staff in opposite directions between his two white knuckled fists and took a batter's stance. With a powerful swing, he hit Neil directly in the stomach with one end of the staff. Neil's hanging torso swung from the impact. On its return path, Shawn hit him again. Over and over it continued, as Neil became a human piñata. I heard bones breaking and the sound of meat being tenderized. Shawn switched from swinging the staff horizontally to hammering it down on Neil's face. Neil's skull was crushed in, creating a cylindrical trough split down the middle. I was reminded of Gina's face getting punched in the same way. Shawn turned to me.

"Do you get it yet?" he asked.

Before I could answer him, the husk of human flesh and bones that used to be Neil started to shake. It twisted from side to side and the same buzzing kazoo sound came from within him. Shawn took a step back to face me and cocked the staff high on his shoulder. With one final powerful swing, he hit Neil in my direction. Neil's abdomen exploded, sending a thousand screaming spiders flying out towards me. As they flew at me, Shawn screamed one word.

"STAAAAAAAAAAANFOOOOOOOOOOOORD!"

I woke up.

Chapter 25

I sat alone in the train station's parking lot before driving home. It took three tries for my shaking hand to insert the key into the ignition. I was confused. What did this mean? Shawn could not have killed Neil because I had him tied up in my basement. Unless he had escaped. The longer I thought about it, the more paranoid I became. Maybe Shawn had broken free while I was at work and killed Neil to get back at me. Fear and panic tightened around my heart. Sweat poured down my face, stinging my eyes. I fumbled with my seat belt, started the car, and sped home.

By the time I got home, I anticipated a full brigade of law enforcement officers at my house, guns drawn, snipers in the trees, ready to take me out on sight for kidnapping. As I gasped what short shallow breaths I could, I turned into the driveway to meet my doom and was greeted by the faded yellow blank face of my garage door. I gave it a relieved nod and proceeded into the house. I was safe.

After mixing a strong cocktail of one part vodka and two parts more vodka, I cautiously walked down the basement stairs. Shawn sat right where I had left him, strapped to an old folding chair with duct tape, hands behind his back. I had first taped his ankles together, then bound them both to the left leg of the chair. I had considered taping each ankle to a separate chair leg, but thought it would allow him to escape by waddling away. Next, I had tightly wrapped one long piece of tape around his head five times, making sure to cover his mouth in the process. I didn't want to hear anything the mother fucker had to say. Then finally, sticking each of my pointer fingers into the center of the tape roll, I had wrapped the remaining tape around the chair in tight circles, each revolution sealing his body and his fate closer to that chair. It was secured to a support beam in the middle of the room with a heavy chain and an old gym lock I had found.

He was awake, but groggy as if he had recently come to. He looked at me through pleading eyes. I could tell that he recognized me, the house, and the helplessness of the situation. His left ear was red, the source of the dried blood that ran down his neck. His right cheekbone was a swollen black and purple mound. Above his right eye it looked like someone had slit open the end of his eyebrow and inserted a golf ball.

I drank my drink and just stared at him. So far, everything had worked out according to my plan. Now came the part where I made him pay for what he had done to my wife and my friends. He killed my wife. My wife. The realization hit me like a punch to the stomach, as if I truly understood it for the first time. This man in front of me took away the woman I loved and changed my very being. This cock sucking dirtbag piece of shit. The anger started rising inside of me as the alcohol hit my system. I threw my empty glass against the wall.

"Why the fuck did you do it?" I yelled at him.

There was a look of fear in his eyes and a muffled, "Hmm hmmm?" It could have been "Do what?" or "I'm sorry" or anything I wanted it to mean. I chose it to mean "Fuck you," so I slapped the golf ball in his face. I felt it squish under my palm.

"I asked why the fuck you killed my wife, you piece of shit." I spat in his face, the alcohol in my saliva disinfecting his cuts.

"Hmmmm hmmm hmm!" he replied, each muffled word rising in pitch while decreasing in length. His head started to shake from side to side, attempting to indicate the negative use of the word "Hmmm."

I responded to his answer with a solid punch to the face. Blood and snot poured out of his nose; tears poured out of his eyes. His head was still shaking as he made the chair jump, trying to make his answer heard. His voice rose to a high-pitched squeal like a pig's, which was exactly what he was. So I let him know.

"You sound like a fucking pig. Squeal, little piggy!" I shouted at him, each word a verbal assault accompanied by a physical one. Right fist, left fist, repeat. I hammered out months of sadness through aggression. Soon his entire face was slick with his own blood. My knuckles were stained with it. I stopped to catch my breath.

"So what happened, you fucker? Why would you break into my house and kill my wife? What did she ever do to you, you fucking psychopath?"

His shoulders shuddered with heavy sobs as he tried to extract oxygen through bloody mucus. His head still shook "no" but it had slumped down, no longer looking at me, his chin touching his chest. I took the sudden change in his head placement to mean that he disagreed with my last allegation. Or maybe he was just about unconscious.

The police hadn't said anything about forced entry on the night of Vicky's death. There were no broken windows or jimmied locks. "You did break in?" I half asked, half told him. All I could hear was bubbling snot forced in and out of his nose and that stupid high pitched squeal starting again. "Quit fucking crying. I'm trying to think." Was he already there that night? Had he been invited in? Had Vicky let him in? That felt more correct. I came to a new conclusion.

"Were you sleeping with my wife?" My voice returned to speaking volume for the moment. The chair resumed jumping and his shaking intensified as his eyes widened. The squealing tapered off into a whimper and the tears in his eyes were no longer from the physical abuse. I stepped back and stared at him through narrowed eyes, trying to process this new information that somehow wasn't entirely new. I felt a distant tug of recognition trying to remember something.

"Were you sleeping with my wife?" I asked again. I entertained the idea. I had been working an insane amount of hours and the long commute hadn't made it any better. She was always my best friend, but was I really hers? Memories unlocked and flooded into my mind. Silent nights not speaking to each other. Meals eaten alone while she sat in another room. The glass she had thrown at me after I put it in the sink instead of the dishwasher. Every interaction, an event, a struggle to get from start to finish. She had even resorted to sleeping in a different room. At the time, I had refused to see these facts for what they were. My excuse was that these were just the trials and tribulations of marriage. How did I not remember this? I had told my mind to ignore the signs. I had convinced myself that she really did love me, that she would never cheat. My mind now told me otherwise. Had I really blocked it all out? My head began throbbing. I needed another drink.

I ran upstairs to get a drink and to think this through. So Vicky wasn't a perfect angel; she was human. That didn't stop her from being the woman I loved, my best friend and life companion. I had tried to show my love as best as I knew how, but sometimes it wasn't good enough. Every relationship went through ups and downs. Had she really run to the arms of another man? There was a familiar sting in my heart, like an old knife reopening a wound that had partially been healed over with lies. I hated cheaters. They were just as bad, if not worse than murderers. With murder, the person dies completely. With cheating, the person cheated on was forced to live with the pain the cheater created, emotionally dead but still physically alive.

Alternate scenarios played out in my head a thousand times in the passing minutes while I sat there. Maybe she had realized her mistake and had tried to end it with Shawn. I could have forgiven her if she really did love me. Maybe Shawn had gotten jealous, gone crazy, and killed her. And then to hurt me even more, he killed the only friends I had. That had to be it. I finished my drink.

I returned to the basement and Shawn was unconscious again, blood drying with the tears and snot on his face. I crossed the basement and ripped open the lid of the brown storage box I hoped held what I was looking for. I pulled out my old college yearbook, my diploma, and a few random pictures of me with people I didn't talk to anymore. Then I found it. The ring I received while riding the pine to the national championships for football in my junior year. Putting it on the middle finger of my right hand, I noticed the gold was tarnished, but I still couldn't help admiring the huge red ruby in the center. It was the most expensive thing I never earned. I then transferred my wedding ring to my right hand and grabbed a solid steel wrench from my toolbox in the corner. I walked back across the basement and faced Shawn again.

"Rise and shine, mother fucker!" I screamed and

swung the wrench down. I felt his entire cheek bone disintegrate from the blow. He woke up, eyes screaming in pain, the duct tape over his mouth pushing out and sucking in rapidly with each gasping breath he took. The blow had torn his left cheek apart, leaving a flap of skin hanging over the entire side of his now sagging face.

I stepped back, momentarily admiring my work, and then drove my fist into his stomach. I heard his ribs crack with the satisfying snap heard in lobster commercials on TV. How refreshing. Burning liquid hit my forehead and dripped into my eyes. I looked up and saw vomit spewing out from around the duct tape covering his mouth like a thumb over a garden hose of bile. I considered letting him choke to death but didn't think that was quite fitting enough. Not yet.

I ran back to my toolbox, grabbed another roll of duct tape and a razor blade. I pushed the razor blade out with a click of my thumb. The shortest distance between two points is a line, so I calculated the quickest way to remove the tape was to slice one straight down the right side of his face, starting just under his bruises and ending at his chin. The hanging duct tape balanced the hanging flap of cheek on the other side of his face. I admired the symmetry. I ripped the rest of the tape from his mouth. He started babbling nonsense as he finished spitting up the rest of his most recent meal, my friends, right at my feet.

"P... p... p... please. I don't know what you want. I... I... I... I don't know what you think I did, b... b... b... but...."

"Shut. The. Fuck. Up." I spoke each word as I ripped off a new strip of tape and wrapped it around his mouth again. He was no longer going to choke and die and I didn't want to hear his version of the truth. I had mine.

Chapter 26

That Friday on the train, I was truly alone; as anticipated, Neil was missing. The last of my train friends were gone. I sat in my seat, going through the events from the previous night. It was like trying to imagine someone else's dream. Before I left that morning, I had gone downstairs and held the chloroform rag over Shawn's newly deformed face to keep him knocked out for the day. I remembered something about rings and razors. Then I remembered Julie and her fiancé were coming over for dinner.

I did nothing work-related the entire day because I

was too worried about Julie coming over. The house wasn't clean. I had no idea what to cook. Plus there was a tortured man dying in my basement. I hoped they didn't mind chicken and rice. Panic clenched my heart with its icy fingers. Anxiety constricted my lungs, not allowing full breaths of air. I wanted to call off the dinner, but I had already decided that tonight would be Shawn's last night alive and I needed the alibi. The plan was to entertain them for a while, then sometime during the evening go into the basement for another bottle of wine or some other believable excuse, and end it. If I had learned anything from my useless two-dimensional life lessons, it was that cops are very good at pinpointing the exact time of death. Later, when Shawn was either found in a Dumpster, appeared to be the victim of a car accident or something else I hadn't yet thought of, and anything led back to me, then Julie and her fiancé would be able to vouch for my whereabouts in those exact minutes.

"So, are you ready for tonight?" Julie made a point to come over and ask me.

"Sure am," I said, conjuring up the best smile I could. I really meant, "Fuck no."

"Lookin' forward to it," she said and left before another awkward pause could happen. I thought she lingered just a moment too long and wondered what that meant, but told myself I was just imagining things. I left an hour sooner than usual to catch an earlier train so I could get home and finish cleaning. I also needed to get groceries and make sure Shawn couldn't make any noise.

I walked into my house and nearly dropped the plastic bags filled with chicken, rice, and wine out of my arms. I heard blood-curdling screams of pleading and pain, only slightly muffled by the thin wooden door separating the basement from the kitchen. I set down the bags and had a moment of sheer terror as I ran downstairs. How long had this been going on? Had anyone heard his screams? How had he woken up and removed enough of the tape to scream that loudly?

I reached the bottom of the stairs and ran to where I had left Shawn. He had somehow knocked the chair over onto its left side, turned at a perfect ninety degrees from how I had left him. He must have landed on his head as evidenced by the pool of blood and pus all around him, dripping from his face. The fall had torn open the razor cut in his face; the blood must have acted as a lubricant, allowing the tape to slide down from his mouth.

"Shut your fucking mouth, NOW!" I screamed at him. I kicked him in his broken ribs and he let out an even louder cry of pain. I realized that this only created more noise for anyone that might be listening. I forced myself to speak in a calm, rational tone. "Please, stop your screaming before I am forced to hurt you. Again." I didn't think he heard or appreciated my calm request over his mind numbing screams. I picked up the back of the chair and righted him.

"M... M... Man, let me go. I don't know what you think I did, but I d... d... d... didn't do it. I... I don't even know you... Please?" His hysterical attempt to rationalize with me was amusing. No fucking way. It was too late to turn back now. I would have my revenge tonight, for everything this asshole had taken from me. I used more duct tape to cover his mouth. By the time I was done, he was a silver ninja with only his eyes and nose showing through strips of tape. He almost looked like one of those scorpion mummies from my dream. Luckily for me, I had already broken most of his ribs, so writhing legs weren't a threat.

I poured more chloroform over the still damp rag and held it to his face. I watched him drift off into what must be a better place. I wasn't sure if he had awakened before I got home that day because he built up a tolerance to the chemical, but I wasn't about to take any chances of him waking up again while my guests were here. To make sure he was really out, I took a hammer and hit his right kneecap. His bound feet pulled up straight against the tape holding them to the single chair leg, but this was expected. His reflexes were in good condition. He wasn't. But he didn't wake up, so I went upstairs to prepare for my guests.

Chapter 27

I couldn't remember the last time I had cooked an actual meal for anyone. It was most likely for Vicky when she was alive. As I sat there preparing the chicken, I remembered that I really used to love to cook for her. She would always sneak into the kitchen and pick at whatever I was making. "Just to see if it was even edible," she would say to me with a wink and a smile. We both knew it was because she really did like my food and it was her excuse to come into the kitchen. Personally, I liked the idea of taking time out to prepare something specifically for another person. And in a way, I was still doing that for her.

While I was lost somewhere between a flood of memories and a mushroom sauce, the doorbell rang. They were here. More specifically, she was here. I opened the door and it was just Julie.

"Hey... there..." I greeted her, looking around her for her fiancé.

"Hi. Listen, Pete is so, so, so sorry that he couldn't make it. He got really sick at the last minute. I didn't want to cancel so I just came by myself. I hope that's okay? I know how important this is to you." She really meant it was important to her.

"Sure, sure," I replied thinking at least I wouldn't have to stumble over his name the entire evening. Then I wondered why I couldn't remember that his name was Pete. It was such an easy name to remember.

"Are you really sure it's okay?" she asked, turning her face to look into my eyes which had drifted off into the distance thinking about her fiancé's name.

"Oh, right. Yeah, sure, that's fine. Thanks for still coming out. I know it's a long drive, especially by yourself."

She laughed. "I think I can handle a two-hour drive out from the city." If she was that worried about me not wanting her to come by herself, she should have called first before making the journey all the way out here. But I didn't mind; I really needed the alibi.

We looked at each other, smiling, eyes locking for a moment. I invited her in, taking the bottle of wine she had brought with one hand and helping her take her coat off with the other. "I know you said not to bring anything, but I always feel bad coming empty-handed to a person's house."

"Oh, it's okay. The more wine, the better, I always say," I said, actually for the first time.

She looked at me with a tinge of regret in her eyes, possibly thinking that alcohol might not have been the best idea given my recent appearances at work. She shrugged it off, took the bottle back from me and said, "Where do you want it?" I told her to just put it on the counter while I went to hang up her coat.

I thought my plan would still work if it was just her. An alibi is still an alibi. I just needed to slip away for a few minutes, do what I had to do, and get back to her. I hung her coat on the coat rack and walked back into the kitchen. She was staring at the two nail holes in the floor I had never gotten around to filling in, a gaping memory like an open wound. I coughed to announce my return and she snapped up, embarrassed to have been caught looking.

"I just can't bring myself to patch up those holes. It's a terrible memory of her, but I just can't do it." This was one of the few truthful things I said all night.

"Oh, you poor thing. I can't even begin to imagine," she said, rubbing my shoulder, attempting to turn this into a pity party. Maybe this was the reason she had come here by herself; she needed this more than I did.

We entered an awkward silence, waiting for the moment to pass. To hurry it up, I asked, "What do you say we crack open that bottle of wine?"

Her answer was a half smile, half frown; it just made her mouth a straight line and she nodded. I dug through a cabinet I hadn't been in for months and found the wine opening set. Vicky and I had bought it for ourselves at a discount when no one got it for our wedding. A tug of sadness pulled at my heart. The last time I had used this set was our five year anniversary when we got extremely drunk together. The joke that night was that we had gotten some pretty strong cheese, since it couldn't possibly have been the wine. This memory of cheese faded into the image of yellow pus on my basement floor. Fury with Shawn crept in knowing that there would be no more future memories. I longed to excuse myself for a few minutes to finish the job.

Julie must have thought I was staring too long at the wine opening set. "You know how to use one of those or do you need some help?"

"Nope. I got it." I proceeded to open the wine bottle with all the professionalism of a connoisseur. "First, tilt the bottle for presentation and open on an angle. Never set the bottle flat and open it. It's just tacky. Approach the cork with the corkscrew at an angle to ensure your first twist drives the screw into the exact center of the cork. This prevents the cork from breaking while ensuring it will pull out completely. Two and a half twists in and pull the cork out. Done."

"Well, I'm impressed. Did you take a wine class or something?"

"I got *Wine Drinking for Dummies* some Christmases ago and that always stuck with me." I thought it was amazing how you could remember the littlest things and completely forget about the bigger ones.

"Very professional, regardless of where you got it from."

I poured two glasses of the Pinot Noir, noting how similar it looked the puddle on my basement floor, and set them down in front of us on the kitchen table. "Here's to good times and better friends." My toasts were never my strong point. Vicky once helped me through a toast I was asked to give for my dad at his sixty-fifth birthday party. And by "helped" I mean she didn't laugh when I raised my glass, looked at my father and said, "Here's to good times and a better father." I was always toasting to good times. Maybe it was just wishful thinking.

Our glasses clinked and we both took long drinks, each trying to think of the next thing to say. She thought faster than I did, most likely because I was already drunk.

"So, I hope you don't mind me getting a little personal, but how are you doing? Six years we've been working together and I've never seen you like this. It seems like you've just shut down since... since... you know."

"I've been coping well. It's gotten easier as time passes." Not true.

We stared into each other's eyes, a strange vibe occurring that I hadn't felt since Vicky was alive. She sighed, with whatever she wanted to say right on the edge of her lips.

"I... don't know how to say this, but...."

The oven timer went off, ending whatever trance we were about to fall into before it began. We both shook our heads, as if waking up from a dream.

"Chicken is ready. I hope you're hungry." True and not true. The chicken was ready, but I didn't really care if she was hungry. My mind was consumed with finishing the job in the basement.

"You know it," she said, seeming almost happy that something had stopped her from continuing.

I refilled our glasses with the rest of her wine and brought over two plates of chicken and rice, mixed together with an old secret family recipe, which was really a can of

him. The picture of Vicky and me at Yosemite Park. Our wedding night. Arguing with her the final morning I saw her alive. My best friend and lover for over ten years. Rob and Gina, fighting but in love. Frank, a man who chose to ignore his pain, keeping a positive attitude through a worn down life. Sheila, eating herself to death, trying to find comfort in food as a way to deal with her pathetic, ugly life. Neil, hoping to remain young and desirable in anyone's eyes despite growing old alone. This was for all of them. For who they were, what they had become, and what they meant to me. I pressed the blade against the left side of his neck until it popped through his skin and disappeared. Then I dragged it slowly across to the other side. The shortest distance between my pain and redemption is a straight line.

From behind, I held his forehead with my arm and tilted his head back to avoid being squirted with blood. Shawn remained unconscious the entire time. After the initial geyser dissipated, blood escaped his body in red streams synchronous to his deep breaths. I sat there in silence, just holding him in his last final moments. When his breathing stopped completely, he was dead.

I grabbed a bottle of wine and headed upstairs just as the toilet flushed.

Chapter 29

We met in the hallway at the same time, she walking back to the kitchen, me coming up from the basement. "Are you okay? You're sweating..." she asked me, reaching up to touch the beads of perspiration on my forehead.

"Oh, yeah, fine. I, uh, just ran down the stairs to get this," I said as I raised the bottle. "Just need to catch my breath." But the real reason I was sweating was panic. I had been expecting some cathartic release after killing Shawn; I had been counting on it. But there was nothing. I still felt empty inside. I should have felt happiness after putting the person that killed my wife and my friends to rest. I chalked it up to having a corpse hidden in my basement and hoped that once the body was gone, I would feel the release. "Do you want to go sit in the living room?"

"Sure, but I don't want much more wine, especially if I have a two hour drive home... Unless of course..." she began, her right hand caressing my left arm. I jerked away from her, immediately regretting my overreaction. She was probably just concerned. She quickly brought her hand back to her side.

We walked into the living room with full glasses of wine and she proceeded to talk. About what, I didn't know, as my mind raced a mile a minute in a thousand different directions. I had just killed a man. But that man had killed my wife, so it was justified. But it was still murder, so that was not okay. But that man had killed my friends, so it was okay. I felt like throwing up.

I interrupted Julie mid-sentence and excused myself to go to the bathroom. I needed to pull myself together. I grabbed the little flask I kept hidden in the medicine cabinet for such occasions and drank half of it in one long calming gulp. It helped me to think it all through logically. The world started to spin. Vicky was all I had in my life. After she was taken from me, I only had my train friends. And Shawn had taken all of them from me. He had taken everything. He needed to be stopped and the police had been of no help. I had to do it. Whether you called it murder or revenge, it was justified; it was the correct thing to do. As I set down the empty flask, I felt better. Calm.

I walked back to the living room and sat next to Julie on the couch. "So where were we?" I asked with a smile.

"I was telling you about how at work sometimes..."

Her rambling forced me back into my own thoughts, set to autopilot again. I snapped back when I felt her hand slowly moving up my inner thigh, massaging it just enough to be sensual. As if there was any other type of action that could take place in that area.

"I was just hoping it wasn't too soon, you know?" she asked, her breathing suddenly deepening. I had missed something. She leaned over and put her mouth on mine, her lips trying to part mine. Her tongue felt like a snake's, darting in and out and around my sealed mouth, looking for a way in.

I grabbed both of her shoulders and firmly pushed her away. "Julie. What the heck are you doing?"

"I... I... I thought you wanted this?" she asked, trying to turn it on me.

"What are you talking about? What makes you think I would want this?" With everyone close to me dead, including the body in the basement, I wanted nothing to do with "this."

"Well, for starters, I was the first person you ran to when you guys started having problems..."

I had told her all of that? I felt a tug of recognition.

"And all of the late night flirting between us. The days we didn't even have to stay late, but we did. I see the way you look at me."

I think she had confused my empty-on-the-inside look for one of lust.

"Julie, listen. I'm flattered, but I did love my wife regardless of what you might have thought..."

"No, you didn't! You said, 'It used to be great, blah,

blah, blah, but lately we've drifted apart,' and you guys never talked, you didn't even sleep in the same room."

"B-b-but that doesn't mean I didn't love her. I mean, every couple goes through..."

"What are you talking about? You even told me she was cheating on you. Do you remember what you told me, how you felt about cheaters? And she was doing it. She was cheating." There was fire in her eyes.

That couldn't have been real. How did I not remember any of this?

The room spun. "No. That isn't true. She was my best friend and the woman I loved. She wouldn't have done that to me."

"Well, she did. Why are you suddenly denying this? You were at work late, with me by the way, and came home and said she smelled like wine and cologne."

Just thinking of what that would smell like made my heart sink. But that couldn't be true. Not my Vicky.

"You told me the worst thing in the world was a cheater and that they should all burn in hell. You told me this in tears while I held you. Me. I was the one who was there for you while that whore was running around with that carpenter, Shane or Shawn or whoever."

I felt like I had been punched in the heart at the mention of that name. Shawn was dead. But Shawn was a dentist, not a carpenter.

"Night after night, I would hold you while you went on and on about it. How you would show her. How you and I should get together and that would show her."

"Did we ever.... you know?" Was I a hypocrite?

"No. We both wanted to, but you stuck to your goddamn morals about cheating. I never understood it. I started to think it was me, because no man could have been that decent to a person who was doing such a terrible a thing to him. So was it?"

"Was it what?" Everything was blurry, Julie, the room, my memories.

"Was it me? She's gone now and it's just us. You're no longer constrained by your stupid ethical cheating rules. So it must be something. You've been brushing me off all night. Is it me?"

"No, it's not you, Julie, I just..." I just couldn't

remember any of this.

"You just what? You have me here all to yourself, I'm practically throwing myself at you, and what? Still nothing. Were all those late night talks just a plan to get back at her? You told me it was more than that. That you could see yourself with me, if it weren't for her."

I said that? How could I have said that?

"It's too soon. I loved her." This was true; I loved Vicky with all my heart. Right?

"Bullshit! You didn't love her. You even told me you hated her! I believe the exact words were, 'she's a cheating lying bitch that should rot in hell.'" Julie's voice was getting louder and louder.

She had to be making this up. It was the only explanation. "Well, what about whatshisname, Pete? Wouldn't you be cheating on him? Did you think I would like that? Did you consider that part of your plan? Did you even tell him about tonight or was it just another lie?" I was starting to get pissed off. I finished my wine, went to the kitchen, and grabbed a bottle of Stoli from the cabinet.

"As I've told you a hundred times, it wouldn't be

cheating if I ended it with him." She started to cry, but I couldn't tell if they were tears of sadness or anger. I didn't really care. "Why don't you love me all of a sudden? Things could be perfect for us."

I felt very disoriented and confused. The room was a blur behind Julie. I could only focus on her to keep from falling over.

"FUCK YOU!" she screamed at me. "You said you were falling in love with me. Now that your cheating wife is out of the picture, you should be with me!"

Something snapped.

"You're just another dirty fucking whore." The world was as slurred as my words were. My head swam with mixed up memories of people, time, and space. Shawn, Julie, Vicky. "You are a cheater and a fucking liar!" I was screaming. My focus was gone. Julie shrunk back just a little under the wrath of my stupor.

"Don't you dare talk to me like that! I know how you felt about her cheating and I'm nothing like that!" Her voice was close to hysterics. Tears ran down her face in rivers, dripping onto the hardwood floor.

"You know nothing about what the fuck I want or who the fuck I want." The world was coming at me and pushing away from me. "I can't believe you fucking slept with him, you cheating filthy slut."

Past the tears in Julie's eyes was a look of utter confusion. "What the hell are you talking about?"

"I'm going to teach you a fucking lesson." I had no idea where this came from; I had no control over my words or my actions. I was again on autopilot, watching myself from somewhere else. Observing but unable to interact, like a dream.

She started backpedaling into the living room. "Wha... wha... what did you j-j-j-just say?"

I stood up.

"I said, I'm going..."

I walked back to the kitchen.

"...to teach you..."

I turned to her, picking up an empty wine bottle.

"...A FUCKING LESSON!"

I hurled the bottle at the stove, where it shattered into a thousand pieces.

I was gone.

been so greatly distorted that they needed to identify him through dental records. I jerked up out of my half sleep at this news and my body screamed at me for it.

"Listen, I know we only met at... um... your wife's... uh," he said, his voice monotone from shock.

"Funeral reception," I finished for him. "Yes, I remember." I now felt completely sober for the first time in months. Julie was gone. The reality took a moment to sink in.

"Well, I just know Julie talked an awful lot about you and since the... uh, a few months ago, you guys have gotten close. I just wanted to let you know myself."

"I don't even know what to say, Pete. I'm so sorry." I couldn't believe it. I was in total shock.

"I just... Do you....Well, do you have any idea what she would have been doing out in the suburbs with that guy? And do you have any idea who he might have been? Had she ever mentioned another man?"

It turned out she hadn't told him anything about the night before. The entire dinner was a set-up from the beginning, the whole "Pete is sick" thing had been an excuse. I could have told him the truth. That we had dinner, a nice conversation, she made a move, I rejected it and she left. But I couldn't do that to him. I had no idea who the guy was that she was found with, but it bothered me that she would even think to do such a thing. I hated cheaters and she knew how I felt about them. My rejecting her was the very reason she had left my house. I was confused as to why she met with someone after leaving my place.

"I'm sorry, Pete. I have no idea. The last time I saw her was at work." From one widower to another, this was a good lie.

We talked for a few more minutes, long enough for him to give me the funeral and wake information and then I put the phone back on its charger. When the light on the phone's base went from red to green, it was like a traffic light for my tears. It was almost like losing Vicky all over again. Julie and I were just friends, but in the short period of time after Vicky's death, she had become my closest friend. And now she was gone too. It wasn't fair. I was alone again.

Chapter 32

That Monday I got on the train again, not to go to work, but to say goodbye to a dear friend. I woke up later than I intended to so I took a later train. It turned out that this later train ran a new express route to the city, arriving just about the same time as my usual train. In fact, it would buy me about twenty extra minutes in the morning if I were to start taking it. I sat in the single row on the top, not facing anyone. I didn't feel like being around people I don't care about who don't care about me.

I sat there in the same daze I had been in since

Saturday, looking out the window, thinking about nothing. Since the train ran express, there were fewer stops and the world was just one big blur, moving too fast to even see where I was. This made me sick after a while, so I turned my attention to the car. A whole car full of complete strangers, with their own happy lives, oblivious to the misery of mine.

On the lower level, I saw an obese woman with gray hair wrapped in a bun eating about a week's worth of calories and fat from a McDonald's bag. She sat next to an older gentleman with an earring and a newspaper. They had just finished discussing how great this new express train was for their commute. The headline next to the older gentleman's gaudy golden ring on his hand read:

"Two Dead in Fatal Car Crash"

Local dentist, Dr. Richard Griffin and Numbers Analyst, Ms. Julie Scarbough both perished in a tragic car accident this past Saturday. The couple was traveling southbound together around one o'clock a.m. in Ms. Scarbough's car...

Then the paper folded over and I couldn't read any more from where I sat. It was just as well. I turned away in disgust at the bloody picture accompanying the article. I never had a stomach for that kind of thing and I couldn't believe they'd publish that filth right on the front page.

Behind the obese woman sat a friendly looking guy in his late forties, balding with deep wrinkles. He was reading the same paper as the older gentleman. He had just finished apologizing for not letting the obese woman and older gentlemen know he went on vacation a week or two ago. All three of them seemed like a close knit bunch of friends. I didn't care. Aside from those three, there were rows and rows of people, all so close but not knowing or caring about each other. It was extremely disheartening. I closed my eyes and rested my head on the window, not wanting to be stuck here alone in a train full of so many strangers, yet not quite wanting to be a part of the blur outside. For the moment I would take comfort in just resting inside of my own head. Sitting in blackness from closed eyes, I heard a couple a few seats behind me arguing quietly about dishes or some other inconsequential thing that only lovers could argue about. The man sounded quite smug. I drifted off into a dreamless sleep.

Chapter 33

I walked into Julie and Pete's house. I knew from experience that it used to be a home. I passed through a cloud of solemn background chatter, full of sorrow and pain. The buffet table was to the right, holding comfort food for anyone looking to fill their emptiness. I had no desire to eat. I saw Pete standing in the back of the living room by himself, trying to hide the tears running down his face. Like people were going to judge him for crying. I made my way across the room through the maze of people, throwing out obligatory remarks to anyone who got in my way.

"Hi, Pete. I'm so, so, so sorry. Julie was such a dear friend," I said while extending my hand to take his. He surprised me by bypassing my hand and wrapping his arms around me in a giant hug.

"Thank you, Stan. I feel like I'm falling apart here. I know this can't be easy on you either, with your wife having so recently..."

"The least of your worries at this time, Pete," I said while awkwardly returning the hug. There was some comfort in physically touching someone going through the same thing I had. Nothing could ever change that. In that moment I felt a bond stronger than I had felt in months. Some basic part of me was no longer completely empty.

"I... I... I... just c-c-c-can't... Sh-sh-sh-she was everything to me. I couldn't ever imagine this hap-p-p-p-ening." He was now openly sobbing on my shoulder. "Tell me... does it ever get easier?"

I thought about this question for a moment before answering. I really did. I chose not to lie like I had with Julie's whereabouts.

"No. It doesn't get easier. You will wake up every day

for the rest of your life feeling this pain." At least I was honest. "The trick is learning how to deal with it; that pulls you through your remaining days."

"How do you deal with it?"

There was some recognition as I disengaged from our hug and looked right into his eyes, my hands still resting on his shoulders.

"Pete, the mind is a very powerful thing. You'd be surprised at how much it can get you through."

The End

Acknowledgments

To all those who read this book in its early stages, I wholeheartedly thank you. I appreciate you taking the time in your busy lives to help me mold my story into what it is today. Every thought, feeling, point of confusion or clarity was noted and addressed to the best of my ability.

Four people I must thank by name are Dina Darling, Emily Schein, Rachel Garrison, and Jeff Dometita. Without these four this book would not exist. Dina has been a constant supporter, encouraging me to pursue my writing and see it to the end. Emily relentlessly edited and refined the words contained in this book. It reads exceptionally better as a result. Rachel is the genius behind the artwork and is truly an amazing artist. She got inside the book and inside my head to create a cover that perfectly captures the essence of the story. Jeff selflessly took on all the effort to format both my words and the artwork to make sure the end result was what I had envisioned from the start. To all of you, I am eternally grateful.

Made in the USA
Lexington, KY
05 April 2018